AGAINST THE MACHINE

A Bill Blake Novel

Rob Jones

ISBN: 9798796249734

Other Books by Rob Jones

The Joe Hawke Series
The Vault of Poseidon (Joe Hawke #1)
Thunder God (Joe Hawke #2)
The Tomb of Eternity (Joe Hawke #3)
The Curse of Medusa (Joe Hawke #4)
Valhalla Gold (Joe Hawke #5)
The Aztec Prophecy (Joe Hawke #6)
The Secret of Atlantis (Joe Hawke #7)
The Lost City (Joe Hawke #8)
The Sword of Fire (Joe Hawke #9)
The King's Tomb (Joe Hawke #10)
Land of the Gods (Joe Hawke #11)
The Orpheus Legacy (Joe Hawke #12)
Hell's Inferno (Joe Hawke #13)
Day of the Dead (Joe Hawke #14)
Shadow of the Apocalypse (Joe Hawke #15)
Gold Train (Joe Hawke #16)
The Last Warlord (Joe Hawke #17)

The Avalon Adventure Series
The Hunt for Shambhala (Avalon Adventure #1)
Treasure of Babylon (Avalon Adventure #2)
The Doomsday Cipher (Avalon Adventure #3)

The Hunter Files
The Atlantis Covenant (Hunter Files #1)
The Revelation Relic (Hunter Files #2)
The Titanic Legacy (Hunter Files #3)

The Cairo Sloane Series
Plagues of the Seven Angels (Cairo Sloane #1)

The Harry Bane Thriller Series
The Armageddon Protocol (A Harry Bane Thriller #1)

The Jed Mason Series
The Raiders (Jed Mason #1)

The Bill Blake Series
An action-thriller series for fans of
Jack Reacher and Jason Bourne

The Operator (Bill Blake #1)
Against The Machine (Bill Blake #2)

The DCI Jacob Mystery Series
The Fifth Grave (A DCI Jacob Mystery)
Angel of Death (A DCI Jacob Mystery)

Visit Rob on the links below
for all the latest news and information:

Email: robjonesnovels@gmail.com
Twitter: @AuthorRobJones
Facebook: http://bit.ly/RobJonesNovels
Facebook Reader Group: ADVENTURE HQ
Website: www.robjonesnovels.com

“All I care about right now is escaping the machinery of justice.”

Albert Camus, ‘The Stranger’

ONE

Gare du Nord, 10th arrondissement, three kilometres north of central Paris, France. The City of Light. Beams of light, streaming in through the train shed's soaring cast-iron and steel roof like inside a cathedral as I closed in on my target. He was still too far away to catch, weaving in and out of groups of travellers waiting to board a Eurostar train as he neared the end of the platform.

Short guy, bleached denim jacket with a hood down over his shoulders. Frayed black jeans and scuffed black docker boots pounding on the concrete floor. Hair was black, tight curls. Silver braided wheat chain loose down on the left wrist, sliding up and down as he ran, its metal glinting in the station's overhead globe lights high up on the shed roof. And fast, too. Moved like the wind.

I was faster and caught up with him by the time he reached the end of the locomotive. The enormous cab unit's traction motor was rumbling as we burst past. I closed in, readying to reach out and grab the back of his jacket when a woman rounded the corner of the cab and rolled a baby stroller in between us. I smashed into it and knocked it over on its side. The baby tumbled out onto the flagstones and screamed. The panic-stricken mother cried out in shock and reached down for her child. I was already on my way, leaping over the upturned stroller and struggling to regain some balance as I picked up speed in pursuit of the fleeing man, but he was gone.

I pulled up and took a second to scan the busy platform. A boiling sea of people. Hundreds of travellers were milling around, some casual with hands in pockets and scarves around their necks, others in suits pulling expensive rolling luggage behind them and staring up at the departure boards. A woman with a bunch of fresh flowers was busy staring out into the mob trying to find someone, but no sign of whoever it was. No sign of my target, either. Then I saw it in the corner of my eye. A scuffle and another woman screaming. I turned and saw the man in the denim jacket pushing his way past a young couple and heading for one of the station's main exits up ahead.

He'd found his second wind. I took off after him again, counting at least a dozen CCTV cameras following the chase, swivelling their metal heads and tracking us both. He now turned left and approached an exit. He blew past a busy tourist information kiosk and charged through some double glass doors, roughly pushing a man with a young child out of the way. Standing beside them, the boy's mother shouted at him and reached out for her crying child as the father curled his hand into a fist and waved it in the air. The woman released her child and was already reaching for her mobile phone.

People turned and stared. I pushed them out of my way and continued after the target. He emerged from the station and ran out into a diffused, drizzly late afternoon daylight. Traffic and pedestrians all over the Place Napoleon III. Ahead of me, he vaulted over two rows of concrete anti-terror crash barriers and darted through a jumble of gridlocked cars and buses. I kept my eye on his hooded denim jacket and tracked him onto the west side of the Boulevard de Denain. He disappeared for a second under the red striped awning of a quiet café at the north end of the street, but then slid back into sight.

He was still running. Young and fit and heavily incentivized, I guessed. In and out of my line of vision like a salamander fleeing the talons of a hungry hawk. At a small bar a little beyond the café, he kicked a wooden chair out of the way then made his way over the street, flicking his head around to check if he had lost me or not. He was out of luck. He had not. He gauged the distance between us and accelerated, pounding down the boulevard and hanging a tight left around the next corner.

I was losing him. Like any city, Paris was a rabbit warren. Let a guy like this out of your sight for a heartbeat and he's gone for good, especially if he knows the streets. I had to guess this guy knew the streets, so I accelerated to make the corner before I lost him. When I got there and rounded the corner, he was already halfway over a broad junction. A driver swerved to avoid hitting him and skidded to a halt in the middle of the junction, honking his horn and waving a clenched fist out of the window.

The guy never looked back. He sprinted down Rue la Fayette and then slipped out of sight down a side street halfway down the road. I was there just seconds later, but he was gone. Again. I pulled up to a stop, my heart beating like a jackhammer. Typical Paris street. Sixteenth Century Renaissance houses with gabled roofs lining both sides. Plane trees. Cars parked bumper to bumper on both sides. Parking tickets stuffed under windscreen wipers in little plastic bags. A handful of people walking down the pavements with mobile phones clamped on their ears. A woman in a fur coat, leading a pink poodle and checking her makeup in a compact mirror. The point was, no one was turning to see why a man was sprinting down the road in broad daylight. That meant he hadn't gone past them.

Most of the buildings were residential. There was a small boutique and maybe a couple of cafés at the far end. Too far away. If the reaction of the other pedestrians wasn't enough, the distance to the end of the road sealed the deal. He'd never have got all the way down there in the time it took me to get to my current position. He had to be closer. I had to take a punt on where he went up at this end of the street. A third of the way down on my right was a small bar called Le Petit Hôtel.

I crossed the street and scanned inside through the window before pushing open the door. A tall man in a white shirt and black waistcoat was behind the bar. He had a neatly clipped hipster beard and nodded at me and offered a business smile. Casually asked me what I wanted, but when he spoke his eyes flicked to a door behind him. That was the tipoff I needed. I said nothing and made my way over to the door. He raised his hands and told me to move back, so I pushed him away hard and he fell down. I stepped to the door and opened it. On the other side was a short corridor leading to the toilets. The gents' door was swinging to a close.

I walked over and kicked the door open to find the guy in the hooded denim jacket halfway through an open window above one of the sinks. I grabbed his legs and pulled him back inside. His upper body fell forward and his face smashed into the porcelain basin splattering blood up the white tiles. He growled in pain and kicked out at me, pushing me back and scrambling to his feet in one movement. He spun around, chest rising and falling hard with the deep breaths he was taking. Then he pulled a knife on me. I made some calculations about the guy's fitness, centre of mass, dominant hand. His exhaustion after the chase was cancelled from the equation by my exhaustion, but I was taller and heavier and had combat training. Judging by the way he was holding the knife, I guessed he did not, and now he was cornered. So far, so good. But he had an answer and that answer was the flick-knife he had produced from his jeans pocket which he now snapped open along with a snarl.

"Now, you die, stranger."

And he took a step towards me with the blade in his hand.

TWO

I was more interested in the weapon than the attitude. As I drew closer, I saw it was a classic Italian stiletto, maybe Pro-Tech. Milled aluminium body, machined into a beautiful ergonomic curve and at its business end, three and a half inches of cold 154CM steel. I'd seen them before but never used one. At least this way, I had a try before you buy opportunity.

"Who the hell are you?" he asked in French.

"Think of me as a problem."

"You just made a big mistake, Monsieur Problem."

"I don't think so," I said. "I rarely make mistakes, especially big ones."

His eyes scanned the room but there was only one escape and that was the door right behind me so he doubled down on the hard talk. This told me he had little confidence using the stiletto. "This has nothing to do with you, stranger. Whoever you are. You need to get lost or you're going to get killed."

Without warning, I lunged towards him, brought my

arm down hard and smacked the heel of my hand against his wrist, knocking the knife from his grip. It struck the tiled floor with a loud clatter and I managed to sweep it under one of the cubicles with the side of my boot. It came to a rest at the base of a toilet, well out of his reach even with the door open. He looked at it greedily and then reached inside his jacket for another weapon but he never got a chance to pull it on me.

I charged into him, pushing my forearm hard into his throat to shut him up and force him back against the wall, arms pinned behind his back.

"You are out of your depth!" he said.

I said nothing and pushed harder. He started gagging as I put more pressure on his throat. His eyes were already bloodshot, maybe through too much cocaine, but now they were starting to bulge, just like the veins in his neck and forehead.

The barman stepped into the toilets. I couldn't turn my head away from the guy I was pinning against the tiles but I was able to see his face in the mirror above the sinks. The expression on his face told me this wasn't the first time this guy had used his bar as an escape route.

"What have you done this time, Manu?" the barman said in French.

"Nothing."

"I'm calling the police. On both of you."

"No police, please," Manu said.

I said, "Get out or your next."

To his credit, the barman simply shrugged and walked back out of the door. I had to presume the threat to call the police was no bluff and decided to speed things up a notch. I reached into his jacket and found what he had been looking for, a Beretta Centurion.

"Naughty, naughty," I said, tutting. "These are very hazardous to your health."

"You're a dead man!"

I stuffed the gun into the pocket of a big, old leather barn coat I had picked up in London before I fled England. It belonged to an old friend, but now I thought of it as mine. The gun was safe inside it. There was no need to threaten its use here. I wasn't going to shoot him and he probably knew it. Bluffs are best left to amateurs. Instead, I would do things the old-fashioned way. I already had him where I wanted him, after all. "Shut your mouth, Manu. I'm doing the talking now. When it's your turn, I'll let you know. Now, what did that woman back on the platform at the Gare du Nord mean when she said her sister's life depends on me catching you and finding out who you work for?"

He shrugged. "I have no idea. She is obviously a crazy bitch. There are thousands in Paris."

I squeezed harder and he croaked and slowly turned purple. If properly administered, a good chokehold can knock someone out in around ten seconds, more or less. In the case of a blood choke, if the guy you're choking has an adrenaline surge, he might still be pumping on all six cylinders even after you've cut the blood supply and his unconsciousness is already baked into the pie. If you're applying the chokehold to obtain information, the art of it is to give the impression that blackout is imminent while insuring the blood can still flow up to the brain, keeping them conscious. The problem was the angle I was standing wasn't conducive to delivering a blood choke, so Manu was suffering an air choke, where you pure pressure on the trachea area. These are harder to control than a blood choke, and usually cause the victim more pain.

I said, "You won't like it if I make you pass out. When you wake up you'll be hanging upside down in an abandoned warehouse somewhere. Then I'll use a different sort of vocabulary to make you talk."

"You don't who you're toying with, friend," he managed, still purple. "They will stub your life out in the blink of an eye."

"Last chance. What did she mean when she said her sister's life was depending on me getting a hold of you?" I squeezed harder, and now brought my right hand up and pressed my thumb into his left eye socket. "I'll take it out with one push and you spend the rest of your life with a glass eye."

He struggled more but I felt the tension drain from his body. Despite the rage and determination on his face, his relaxing muscles told me otherwise. He was giving in. "All right, all right. Damn it! You're the crazy one, not that bitch!"

"Give me the information I want. Manu… Now. Why did you attack her?"

"It was not an attack. I was sent to warn her."

"Warn her about what?"

"To back off."

"To back off what?"

He paused. The thumb pushed harder.

"Please, no! I will tell you what you want to know, but then you will be a dead man walking. I swear it."

"I'm still waiting."

"She sent a private investigator after my employer. He was snooping around asking questions about her sister."

"What about her sister?"

"Her sister is gone, stranger. Taken."

"You mean kidnapped?"

He nodded. "She is gone forever, believe me. Snatched off the street. She will not be found. She cannot be found. But this woman will not get the message. She keeps asking questions. But when the police filed her disappearance at the back of the cabinet, this crazy bitch hired a private investigator to track her down."

"And you came here today to tell her to call this guy off."

He laughed. "The private investigator is dead. Killed by my employer. I came here today to tell her that she would be dead too if she tries to hire another one. She tried to slap me, so I taught her a lesson. That's what you saw back on the platform."

"What's your surname, Manu?"

"My surname? What has that got to do with anything?"

I pushed harder. "What's your surname?"

"All right. Damn it, all. Manu Badeaux."

"Who do you work for?"

"You'll kill me before I tell you that. The death you inflict on me will be nothing compared with what my employers will do to me if they find out I squealed on them."

"Don't count on it."

He shrugged. "So, kill me."

The woman back on the platform had asked me to track this guy down and get his name. She had said something about her sister's life depending on it. She had cried out for someone to stop him. She was desperate and wouldn't have been thinking straight. I had stopped him and got his name, but it wasn't enough. But I believed him when he said he would never give up the names of his bosses. I decided that whatever was happening between the two of them, she would benefit from as much information as possible. That meant his phone.

"And where is your phone?" I asked.

"I have told you all I know, if..."

Another push. "Where?"

"Inside pocket."

I pulled it out and swiped the screen. "PIN to unlock it."

"C'mon, man..."

Pushed harder on the eye, squeezed harder with my arm, crushing the windpipe. "Now."

He croaked out the code and I typed it in. It worked. Then I drove my fist into his temple and crashed his head against the tiles. The blow knocked him out and his unconscious body slid down onto the floor and fell back into a steel mesh wastepaper basket beside the hand dryer. And now I had to get out of here before the cops turned up. I had something important to clear up. I wanted to talk to the woman back at the station.

THREE

Leaving the chaos of Le Petit Hôtel behind me, I headed back to the Gare du Nord. Turning back into the Place Napoleon, I saw the woman who had asked me to help her. She was outside of the station now, at a small adjacent café, smoking and sitting on a cast iron chair under a red and white striped awning at the far end of the pavement. As I approached, she pushed the chair back a little. Iron scraping on flagstone. The last time I had seen her, she was sprawled out on the platform where the guy now lying unconscious back in the toilets of Le Petit Hôtel had knocked her down with a backhand slap. I had been at the terminus station for less than an hour when she had screamed, arriving just before sundown on a rainy afternoon.

I was cold and hungry and tired. I'd hitchhiked from the ferry port in Calais on board a refrigerated truck heading back to Seville from Coventry after a delivery of oranges, the driver told me in broken English. We got through two packets of Ducados cigarettes and then he dropped me at a fuel station in Bagnolet, in Paris's east end. And then I was at the Gare du Nord with important plans to meet a serious man named Louis Virkler, but in the meantime, I was drinking coffee and eating a sandwich in a pavement café inside the station's famous southern façade.

And that was when I heard the woman scream and saw the man knock her down, right in front of me. She cried out as she fell down and looked over at me as he fled. She told me her sister's life depended on me catching him and getting his name. My experience told me the fear in her eyes was visceral and real. I saw she was burying that fear deep, and not only that, I had also almost finished my sandwich and my coffee was nearly cold, so I decided to get hold of the guy. Do the right thing.

Now, walking over to her, I saw her before she saw me. I approached the table and pulled a chair out. The sound startled her and she jumped in her seat as she turned and took me in. Her right cheek was still red and sore. I guessed she would have some sort of bruising for a few days and maybe even a black eye might develop. You never know. Sitting down opposite her at the small iron table I was able to pay more attention to her appearance.

Average height with brown eyes and dark brown hair floating an inch above her shoulders. Her face was slim and pale with faint freckles across the bridge of her nose. Lipstick the colour of ripe plums and what was probably a pretty expensive perfume, conservatively applied. She wore a taupe trouser suit and a crisp, white blouse. Only jewellery was a pair of sterling silver drop earrings, also modest and conservative. Apart from the beating she'd just got on the platform, she looked like she might have been having a pretty ordinary day.

When she spoke, her calm demeanour broke down a little. Her voice was thin and desperate. "Did you find him?"

I nodded. "Yes."

She frowned but sighed in relief. "What was his name?"

"Manu Badeaux. Does it mean anything?"

She ignored the question. "Are you okay?"

"I'm fine."

"But you have a cut on your cheek."

"It's nothing." I waved it away. It really was nothing. "You should see the other guy. Talking of the other guy, why did he hit you on the platform?"

"You don't need to worry about it. Not now I have the name." She put her half-burned cigarette into an ashtray and reached into her bag and fumbled with her wallet. "I'm sorry I dragged you into this. It's just that everyone else just stood around and watched it happen and when I called out for help, you were the only one who moved. Please, let me pay you for your trouble and don't let me keep you any longer. I don't want you to miss your train."

"Forget about the money and forget about the train. Why did he hit you?"

She paused, then put the wallet back in the bag and the bag back on the table. She picked up her cigarette and took a long, nervous drag. After exhaling, she said, "Are you a cop?"

"No. Would it matter if I was?"

Her jaw clenched for a second, then relaxed. She forced the thinnest of smiles. "Whoever you are, you're not a French policeman. You're not from Paris. That's all that matters."

"And what's so bad about the Paris police?"

She choked down a bitter laugh and dragged on her cigarette again. She exhaled and stared up at the sky like she was searching the heavens for an answer to my question. Another drag and the cigarette was dead, stubbed out in the ashtray. She looked at me again then sipped her coffee from a white ceramic cup with a picture of the Eiffel Tower on the side of it. She put it back down on the table and sighed. Almost as if talking to herself, she muttered, "So that's Manu Badeaux. The man who hit me in the station. That's him. Juliette talked to me about all of this a few weeks ago. That was one of the names she mentioned. Now, at least I can put a face to a name."

She lit a fresh cigarette and waved the packet at me with a question on her face. I took a cigarette and rolled it in my fingers. A moped drove past the café, spewing blue exhaust into the air around our table. The smell of the two-stroke mixed with her cigarette smoke. Behind the Gare du Nord's impressive façade, the sound of one of the locomotives revving up in preparation for its journey north to England echoed up into the sky.

I called a waiter over and ordered a cup of coffee, then I picked up her lighter and lit the cigarette she had offered me. It was still sitting on top of the packet on the table. Gauloises Blondes. I inhaled the smoke and considered walking away. I had somewhere to go and staying in the same place for too long wasn't a great idea. And Virkler was very keen on punctuality and known to get difficult if you kept him waiting, for another thing. Another drag on the cigarette. Filtered, dense, dry smoke with a light, easy flavour and by the time I exhaled, I'd decided to stay and ask another question.

"I'll try another question since you seem to know him. What does Manu Badeaux do when he's not hitting women in train stations?"

A long pause as she thought it over. The second cigarette was now stubbed out only half-smoked. She leaned forward in her chair, elbows on her knees in a classic example of defensive body language, hunching her shoulders in and staring down at her shoes. Then, she looked up at me and caught my eye. "If he's the man Juliette talked about, then he's a small-time pickpocket and drugs runner. Drops heroin and crack cocaine around the city on his Vespa for some very nasty people."

The waiter arrived with my fresh coffee. When he had gone, I said, "You owe these people money?"

She frowned at me, near contempt in her eyes. "No, I do not I owe them money. I am not some pathetic junkie on the streets."

"Not all junkies live on the streets. Plenty of them own luxury apartments."

"I don't own one of those either," she said, going quiet again.

"Why did you tell me your sister's life depended on my getting that guy's name and the names of the people he works for? Badeaux told me someone kidnapped her. Is that true?"

"It's true." After a few seconds, she added, "They have my sister. They have Juliette."

FOUR

I fixed my eyes on her, flicked the ash from the cigarette's tip. "Explain that to me in more detail."

"Juliette, my baby sister," she said, trying not to cry. "They took her away from us."

"Did she owe them money?"

"Why do you keep asking that? You are obsessed with people owing money."

I sipped the coffee. "Owing money to bad people never ends well."

"Maybe so, but she doesn't owe them anything. As a matter of fact, she is a journalist, like me."

"Newspaper?"

"Freelance, and one of the best in France. A little too good, it turns out."

She opened her bag and produced a picture of her sister, handing it to me. Innocent face framed with dark blonde hair. A slightly unconfident smile and clear, honest eyes staring into the lens. She was wearing a white jumper and standing on a beach, hand in the pockets of her blue jeans.

A small black dog was out of focus in the background.

The woman said, "She was undercover, pretending to be a junkie. Doing a story on them, trying to follow the small fish and see if they would swim away and lead her to the big fish. But something went wrong. They must have worked out who she was or what she was doing. I don't know what happened. Either way, they snatched her. I think they're going to kill her."

She broke up and buried her face in her hands, sobbing.

I had noticed how much the act of smoking calmed her, so now I lit a third cigarette for her and handed it over. "Smoke this."

When she took it with trembling hands, I scanned over my shoulder for any sign of any unwelcome company.

"Why do you keep doing that?" she asked.

"Doing what?"

"Looking all over the place every few seconds. Are you expecting someone or are you just a very nervous guy?"

"Don't worry about me. Worry about your sister."

"That's all I've been doing since they took her!"

"And when was that?" I asked because of statistics. After the first seventy-two hours following a kidnap, leads dry up fast and it gets exponentially harder to find people who remember seeing something out of the unusual.

"Yesterday morning."

"Around thirty hours ago. That's good."

"Good?"

"There will be a much fresher trail to follow after just thirty hours. When did you call the police?"

She became vague and hesitant, finding something to look at across the other side of the street nearer to the station. "I never called the police."

Now I knew something was obviously up. First, there was the way she had talked about the Paris police, and now this. Not many people wouldn't go to the police if their sister had been kidnapped, and those in that category would have a very good reason not to call them.

"Why not?"

"Are you sure you're not a cop?"

I drank more coffee. "Pretty sure."

"Then, what are you?"

"I was a soldier."

"Was?"

"That's right, was. Now I'm retired."

"Aren't you a little young to be retired?"

I scanned the street one more time. "Why didn't you call the police?"

"I don't want to talk about it. I don't trust you."

"I just risked my life to help you."

"This could be an act," she said with a petulant shrug.

"I can't help you get your sister back if you won't tell me the truth."

She froze, pale and fragile like a bird. I could see her thoughts whirring behind her eyes. "Why would you help me get my sister back? Who the hell are you, anyway?"

"Maybe I'm someone who can help and you just got lucky today when we were in the same place at the same time."

"I'm not that lucky."

"Today, you were. Why didn't you call the police?"

She sighed. "Okay. The people who took Juliette use the drugs to finance a much bigger operation. The sort of operation that is so big, the police are also involved, if you know what I mean."

I knew what she meant, but I gave none of my thoughts away and kept things simple. "You're talking about serious, organized crime?"

Her mouth turned down at the corners. "And the very worst. Drugs are just on the side. Their main stock in trade is people."

"Traffickers?"

"Women, from Asia into Africa and from Europe into Africa. That's what they do. That's why they took my sister. Juliette was trying to expose them. She told me her story would be explosive, that it would rock not only France but the whole of Europe. The whole of the world."

"Sounds like she got in too deep."

She had been looking away into the middle distance.

When she turned to reply to me, she looked at me with the same, lost faraway eyes. "It's as deep as it gets. Juliette told me she had seen and heard things that made her feel physically sick. Mimi, she said. She calls me Mimi because I am Michelle. Michelle Dupont. Mimi, I need prescription drugs to sleep. This was not the sister I grew up with. We came from a good, stable family. What was she thinking..." her voice trailed away into the surrounding small talk and traffic. "Did Badeaux tell you who he works for?"

"No."

She looked deflated, so I decided to tell her about the phone. "When I asked Badeaux for his name," I said, exhaling the last smoke and stubbing the cigarette out, "I accidentally got hold of his phone, too."

She gave me a doubtful look. "Accidentally?"

"I'm lucky like that."

She looked at me, a mix of horror and hope on her face, as I pulled his battered Samsung out and put it on the table between us. She rubbed her forehead, mouth half-open. "I don't know what this means."

"It means we might have a lead to your sister. The people Badeaux works for might be on here somewhere, either on a contacts list or in a chain of texts or emails."

She reached for the phone and I grabbed her hand to stop her. "Be careful. You might not like what you find."

She hesitated. "But I have no choice! I must know."

I scanned behind me. Still all good. Then I took my hand from hers and leaned back in the chair. "We're looking for his contacts. Go through them and see if you recognize anything."

"But I don't know the PIN."

I read it out to her. "Your friend gave it to me before he fell asleep."

She regarded me with concern in her eyes but quickly disappeared into the phone. After a few seconds, she gasped. She was looking at a picture of a large man with blond hair. "I recognize this man. Juliette showed me a photograph of him a few weeks ago. She talked about him a little. I think he's some kind of bodyguard for the traffickers. His name is Anton Rüdiger."

"Is there an address?"

"Yes, in Montmartre."

Montmartre. We had a lead. For the second time, I vaguely considered walking away. I'd fled unknown dangers in England and put nowhere near enough miles between me and London. On top of this, there was Virkler to consider. The clock was ticking. On the other hand, the Dupont sisters were in serious trouble and had no one else to turn to. After a short silence, I finished my coffee. "My name's Blake, by the way. Bill Blake."

FIVE

Having gained at least part of her trust, Michelle drove me to Montmartre in her car, an old Peugeot with torn cloth seats and a smooth-worn steering wheel pocked with blisters from being left out in the sun. It was in no danger of any further damage today. A steady drizzle had set in and cast a cold, grey light over the entire city. The streets even sounded grey and metallic, dominated by rumbling diesels splashing puddles in the gutters and the depressed sigh of their airbrakes.

We drove in silence as the rain grew heavier, streaking down the windscreen. It was soon a heavy, storm rain and sounded like half-ounce ball bearings clattering on the steel roof above our heads. After a difficult fight through heavy traffic, we finally arrived at the address Michelle had found on the phone. She parked up and pushed back in her seat. I craned my neck and peered up through the driver's window and looked up at the house. Most of the rooms were dark. Behind it, a sky the colour of burnished tin reflected the lights of a thousand rain-slick streets. I heard a heavy wide-body jet roaring overhead, lumbering out of the city on its way to some other land. The day was slowly drawing in.

Michelle pulled a green plastic lighter from her bag, sparked up a cigarette and offered the packet to me. I wiggled one free and took it from the pack. Gauloises Blondes, half-smoked, bright, pale tobacco shreds curling out of the tip of the paper rod.

"You think he'll talk?" she said. "If he's in, I mean?"

"Rüdiger?

She nodded her head.

I slid the cigarette onto my lip and she lit it for me and I took a long, slow drag. Full flavour smoke with a dense body but not as heavy as the richer latakia in the Brunes. Filter muddying the experience, but I felt some tension leave my neck. More smoke. A habit I couldn't shake. I picked it up in Sandhurst and since then it had taken up permanent residence in my life. Research has shown cigarette smoking can reduce life expectancy by up to eight years. Someone once worked out that meant each cigarette shaves off about ten minutes, but then a well-aimed bullet will reduce your life expectancy by one hundred per cent of whatever life you have left in a fraction of a second. I took another drag. I guess I'd already lost another five minutes of my life by the time I gave her an answer.

"He'll talk."

She asked, "How can you be sure? You don't know him."

"No, but I know myself. He'll talk."

She paused, thinking it all through. She took a look up at his house and then sank back into her seat and drummed her fingers on the wheel. "Are you sure this is all right? It seems wrong."

"You want to see your sister again?"

"Of course, I do! But perhaps we should go back to the police, after all. Maybe I could find one who was different, honest. We could give him the information you already got from Manu."

"After everything you already told me, you really think the police would be any different this time?"

She paused. The rain was harder now, striking the roof like rocks and distorting the view through the windscreen. "No, I guess not. It will make it worse."

She stopped talking and tried to make it look like she was just dragging on the cigarette. Then she half turned the ignition to get some power to the electric windows and pushed them both down an inch to let some of the smoke escape.

I checked my watch. I had missed my meeting with Louis Virkler. He was expecting me half an hour ago. He'd get over it in time, but in the meantime, he was known to bear a grudge. He'd done the work and he'd want the money. Letting him down would have consequences, so I decided to give him a call.

A rough, gravelly voice answered after just one ring. "Virkler."

"Louis, how's it going?"

"Where were you, Blake?"

"I got caught up in a thing."

"I don't appreciate being messed around like that. You stood me up, Blake. That's not nice."

"Come on, Louis. Give me a break. Think of all the good times we've had."

"I can't think of any specific ones."

"You owe me."

"No, but you owe me. Remember?"

If there was one thing about Virkler, it was that he was never wrong. I did owe him and he wasn't going to let me forget it. "How can I make things up to you?"

"I'll think of something."

"I know you will. When can I pick it up?"

He started whistling a tune. It was a Chopin nocturne.

"Louis."

"Ah, you want to pick it up. Who says it's ready?"

"Because I was supposed to pick it up earlier and you're Louis Virkler. That's how I know it's ready."

He gave a hollow laugh. "Caught out by my own reputation, is that what you're saying?"

"Something like that."

"You know I'm adding a special surcharge just because

you missed our appointment."

"I thought you might."

"Hey, don't sound so disappointed. You made me stay in and wait for you. You made me miss a date with a beautiful woman. Polish. She is full of promise, Blake. They say she has no limits. Then you mess me around and I miss it all. I was angry at first, but I mellowed when I realised your surcharge would pay for me to take her out to La Tour d'Argent and buy her some roast duck and a few glasses of Piper-Heidsieck. Let me thank you now for being so generous."

"Champagne? I thought you were dry after what happened in Zagreb."

"My willpower comes and goes. I'll expect you tomorrow at six o'clock in the evening at my usual address. If you let me down again, Blake, I will not do business with you ever again. Is that clear?"

"You're a great guy, Louis."

"Au revoir, Blake. And remember what I said about not letting me down."

I hung up and turned to Michelle. She had been sitting with her hands on the wheel, leaning her head casually against the headrest and pretending not to listen to the conversation. I didn't care if she heard it or not. It wasn't a state secret, plus I knew she wouldn't be able to derive very much information from a few quick barbs shared with Louis

Virkler.

"Thanks." I slipped the phone into my pocket. "Unavoidable business."

She shrugged her shoulders. "It has nothing to do with me."

"Listen, I won't be long. I'm just going to check the place out. See if old Rüdiger's around and if so, if he can offer us a little help."

"Take care. These are dangerous people, Bill."

I pulled the handle and climbed out of the car. A sheet of rain lashed my face, driven by a cold wind. Rüdiger's place was just ahead, up on the left. I turned my back on the wind and leaned into the car to tell Michelle to stay put and to drive away if I wasn't back in ten minutes.

I closed the door and tapped on the window, indicating she should lock it. She activated the central locking and watched me walk away. I walked quickly to the house and then broke into a slow jog, keen to make up some time. The house came into view. I vaulted over the front gate and paced up the path to the front door. Before I was at the door, Manu's Beretta was already out and in my hand. I knocked on the door and took a step off to my left. This way more of my body was obscured by the wall when my gun was raised. No reply. I didn't want to hang around and put the door in with my riot boot. It smashed backwards and nearly ripped off its hinges and then wobbled back to the shut position. I kicked it again and moved inside the hall, gun raised into the aim.

SIX

It took seconds to check the downstairs was clear. Then up the stairs to find the same thing. No one was home. I made a light search of the place, looking under beds and inside wardrobes. I found some heroin in a false-bottomed suitcase inside the back bedroom. Classy. Nothing too surprising given the kind of person who owned the house. I turned to go downstairs when I heard a noise. A man cursing downstairs, in French. There was a good chance it was Anton Rüdiger. It was his house, after all. I waited upstairs. It was an enormous house with lots of places to take cover. I figured it would be better to let the fish come to the hook than for me to go wading into the water.

I heard footfall on the stairs. A heavy man, for sure. That linked up to the picture we had seen on Badeaux's phone. Big but not fat. He was halfway up the stairs now, still cursing. From the noise he was making, I took it he thought the damage from my search had been caused by thieves who had long gone with whatever they had raided the house for. I took a step back into the front bedroom, Beretta Centurion still raised. I saw the back of his head now as he made the top of the stairs. I was confident it was Rüdiger from the view I had of the back of him – a thick head of blond hair swept back and held in place with grease, tall and bulky with broad shoulders. He was wearing the same tan leather jacket I had seen in the picture. I took another step back, obscuring my position behind the door frame and watched him as he reached the top of the stairs and turned to walk down the corridor.

Two new pieces of information. First, it was definitely Anton Rüdiger, and second, he was holding a small pocket pistol in his right hand. A Smith & Wesson Bodyguard 380 to be precise. I had guessed he'd be armed. Most people wouldn't go inside their home if they returned to find the front door open, but anyone man enough to go inside their home after the front door had been smashed in would be crazy to do so without some kind of weapon. There was no way to tell if the burglars were still inside or not. For a lightweight handgun, the 380 is a strong and reliable weapon. Made from a high-strength polymer, it's durable and easy to use. Odd choice for Rüdiger, I thought. Big guys like him often have some trouble handling pocket pistols because of the size of their hands. Maybe he'd recently liberated it from someone else. A smaller man or a woman. I didn't care. I knew he was there and what he was armed with. He knew neither of these things about me. Yet.

I stepped out into the doorway, gun pointed at his face. "Drop the gun, Rüdiger."

He didn't flinch. He let the pistol slip from his hand. It tumbled over the bannister rail and landed with a soft thud on the stairs' Persian plush pile.

"Who are you?" he asked.

"I'm a friend of Manu's."

He nodded thoughtfully, as if it might even be true. "I never knew Manu had any friends. Why are you here in my home?"

"Manu told me I needed to talk to you about a problem I have."

"What sort of problem?"

"I'm looking for a friend of mine. She got lost."

He started to relax. His shoulders sloped a little. His large frame deflated. He took a step to his left and leaned on the bannister rail. Nice and casual. Maybe coming home and finding an armed man in his house was ordinary to him. He hadn't looked at the gun in my hand once, just direct eye contact. We were learning a lot about each other. "I regret to tell you, you have been misinformed. I don't find lost people."

"I think today you do."

He cocked his head. "You are with the law?"

"Not the law. Think of me as a freelance problem solver. I told you, I'm looking for a woman."

He smirked. "You can find a woman on any street in Paris."

"Her name is Juliette Dupont."

The smirk evaporated and he tensed. "Who are you?"

"You don't want to find out. If you tell me where Juliette is, you never need to find out."

He ran a hand over his face. He was playing for time. Now he looked at the gun, just for a split second, before bringing his cold blue eyes up to meet mine again. "Would you believe me if I told you I did not know where she is?"

"No."

"That's too bad because it's true."

"You'll have to do better than that. I want a location for Juliette Dupont, now, or I'll put a round through your forehead and I'll sleep just fine tonight. It's not my first time."

He nodded again, in full and complete understanding of his predicament. He seemed to be mulling it over. Then, he got the better of me. Without warning and moving like lightning, he twisted around and vaulted over the bannister rail. I fired a shot which blasted the section of rail he had been holding into smithereens, but he was gone. I heard his heavy bulk crunch down on the stairs and then the sound of him taking two or three risers at a time. No time to get annoyed, I ran down the corridor and turned into the upper landing. He was at the bottom of the stairs having snatched up the 380 en route and now turned and fired it at me. The bullet went wide, ricocheting off the plaster behind my head and blasting a puff of plaster into the air. I fired back, my round chewing into the carpet at his heels. He surprised me again, this time by not running out of the house but turning back inside it and vanishing somewhere on the ground floor.

And I gave chase.

SEVEN

You might say Rüdiger had the home advantage in the empty townhouse. He knew where to go and he went there fast. When I got to the bottom of the stairs, he was already rushing away. With his leather jacket billowing out behind him, he flashed through some open double doors and vanished around the corner of the next room. Large, open spaces, dust sheets, dust motes lit by beams of light scratching in through the shuttered windows. Floorboards, tea chests, chairs stacked upside-down on the dining table. On the floor, I caught sight of a small, used syringe protruding from the side of a packing box. Drugs.

I raised my gun into the aim and moved forward. Slow, measured paces. Clearly, the once luxury home had been taken over by a host of squatters and thieves and anyone else Rüdiger liked to do business with. And clearly, some of them were using heroin. Through the double doors and sweeping the gun around in an arc. Wherever Rüdiger was, he was no longer in this room. He had gone through another door to the right. It was his only play. I made a quick scan of the landscape and saw more drugs paraphernalia. Burnt teaspoons, filthy glass pipes, rubber tubing, tin foil streaked with scorch marks. I flicked another used, bloody syringe away with my boot and headed towards the door.

Outside, a police siren wailed in the evening.

I stepped through the door and found a second staircase leading up to a higher floor. There was nowhere else for him to be so I lifted the gun and craned my neck to see up inside the stairwell. No sign of him. Not even the sound of breathing. Why had he gone back upstairs? I didn't know, but it was my job to find out. I made my way up the old wooden steps. One step at a time, gun firmly gripped in both hands and held out into the aim ahead of me. Three steps up and I was visible to anyone on the landing above. I swivelled around, back up against the white plaster wall and swept the gun up to the landing, half expecting to see Rüdiger looking back down at me with a gun in his hand.

Nothing.

I bounded up the steps and reached the landing. Breathing harder now, my heart going a mile a minute in my chest. Only natural, but I took a second to slow things down. Reduce the adrenaline and stop any tremors going down into my hands and the trigger finger. It's hard to be calm in a situation like this. Hard but essential. I moved forward in the dimly lit landing and stepped inside the only place he could have gone – a narrow door leading into what looked like another staircase going up. I guessed he had headed up to the house's loft space to get out on the roof and make his way down a fire escape ladder or something along those lines.

I had to work fast.

I moved up the steps and reached another door, this time leading out onto the roof. I felt the cold air before I saw the city's evening glow in the crack of the door. I paused a second, took a breath and kicked the door open. Rushing out onto the roof, I had already seen there was no one ahead of me so I swung around and aimed the gun at the brick bulkhead which housed the roof access door. Still nothing, but then a flicker of movement off to the right of the bulkhead. Craning my neck, I saw Rüdiger sprinting along the top of the roof towards the east.

Silhouetted by the rising moon, partly visible through a slit in the clouds low on the horizon, and with the floodlit dome of the Sacré-Cœur off to his left, Rüdiger was making good headway in his bid to reach freedom. I ran after him, gun still in the aim. If he turned and fired a shot at me, I wanted to make sure he was going down before I was. Turned out, he wasn't in the mood to fire and instead slowed to climb down a fire escape ladder, as I had thought. When I reached the edge of the roof, he was already almost at the bottom and obscured by the darkness of a rear courtyard.

I heard his boots smack on the ground and then he made

his way out of the courtyard. I grabbed hold of the rails and made my way down to the ground to see him heading over to another smaller property to the rear of the main house. When I saw a garage door, I guessed he was heading inside to get to a vehicle after he failed to lose me on the roof. The last thing I wanted was a car chase through Paris, especially in Michelle's old Peugeot, so I speeded up and burst into the garage ready to fire.

Inside the garage was dark. I saw an old BMW and a Berlingo parked side by side. The man I had been chasing was standing behind the vehicles, at the back of the space near a workbench. He was breathing hard and looked almost in pain. Hands on knees to steady himself and get his breath back as he stared up at me.

I said, "Hello again, Rüdiger. That was rude."

"Who the hell are you, stranger?"

"Drop the 380 and hands off the knees and into the air where I can see them. Now."

He obeyed, but slowly. I guessed like any man, Rüdiger had his pride. "Who are you? The police?"

"No. I already told you that. I'm just a man looking for answers."

"And what makes you think I can give you these answers?"

"I already told you that, too. I talked to Manu Badeaux earlier today. He said he was a friend of yours. You remember Manu. Black curly hair, leather jacket not unlike yours. Cheap."

He blew out a long breath and nodded. "I know Manu."

"He told me you ordered him to threaten a woman this evening. That's not nice." I was speculating on this, but I was on safe ground. First, Manu could have told me anything. Second, I knew he was playing oily rag to Rüdiger's engine driver. If Manu was out slapping women around, it was only with the blessing of a man like Rüdiger, his handler.

A nervous grin appeared on his face and he started to relax. It seemed that the fog was clearing. "This woman sent you after me?"

"No one sends me anywhere, friend. Why did you send Manu to threaten her?"

"Why should I tell you anything. This is a very loud gun you are holding. No suppressor. I don't think you will fire that in here, not in such a quiet residential area. The neighbours are very respectable people and they will call the police instantly. You will be arrested for murder in minutes."

"I'm not going to shoot you, Rüdiger, but when I'm done with you, you'll wish I had." I put the gun inside my barn coat's inside pocket and picked up a mechanic's hammer from the workbench. "You can take that to the bank."

His eyes widened as he took in the heavy mechanic's hammer in my hand. "Just who the hell are you, anyway?"

"My name is unimportant to you right now. What you need to know is I can and will hurt you very much if you do not tell me what I want to know. I won't enjoy it, but it's business. Now, let's stop beating around the bush. I know you ordered Manu to threaten Michelle Dupont. What interests me is who ordered you to do that? Who is pulling your strings?"

He forced an anxious chuckle. "If you knew that, then you would know why I cannot tell you, stranger. The people who control me are not the sort of people you play with. I cannot tell you anything."

I took a step forward, judging the big hammer's weight and centre of gravity in my hand as I approached him. "Looks like you're in a whole heap of trouble then."

EIGHT

He looked at the hammer with wide eyes as I took another step forward. He reacted by taking a step back, butting up against the garage's back wall. Then, without warning, he opened the BMW's passenger door and tried to slide across into the driver's seat and slam the locks down all one go. He got into the seat and reached for the keys. I swung the hammer and tried to break the window. It shattered the glass but was strong enough to withstand several more blows. With my free hand, reached for the gun in my pocket and fired a shot into the window to finish the job. The explosion was deafening in the enclosed space but had only left a neat spider-web fracture in the glass.

Rüdiger nearly jumped through the car's roof. I used the heavy mechanic's hammer to smash out any remaining glass in the window. Then I pushed the Beretta's muzzle against his temple. He took his hands off the keys and slowly raised them in the air. "Last chance, Anton. What do you say? Save me some time, and also maybe save you fifty thousand euros medical charges?"

He shrugged, maybe even started to look a little confident. "Then, maybe we can do a deal after all."

I kicked the 380 under the Beamer and with the hammer still in one hand, I pushed the Beretta's muzzle harder into his temple. "The deal is easy. Where do I find Juliette Dupont? Last time I ask."

"Please, don't kill me. I beg you."

I reached into the car and took the keys out of the ignition. "Then tell me what I want to know."

"All right, all right. Enough of this bullshit, hein? I was telling the truth when I told you I do not know where she is. I don't get told anything. I run a handful of men like Badeaux, that's it. All low-level stuff but it pays the bills. They tell me nothing at all. But I know who you are talking about. I know who she is. I can tell you that Karim is handling all of the shit to do with the Dupont girl."

"Karim who?"

"Karim Fekir. A Moroccan."

"And how do I find this man?"

"Karim and his friends are like cockroaches. They only come out in the dark, and only when they're hunting for food."

"What do they eat?"

"In this case, the girl you are seeking. She is a young woman whose sale has already been ordered. The deal is done. All the arrangements made. She was asking too many questions and made some very powerful people very anxious. So, they decided to punish her for causing them so much trouble. They are going to take her to the south and then on into Africa, I think. Or maybe the Middle East. I can't remember. Like I said, I get told nothing. I think perhaps she came to the attention of a client in the Middle East. Soon, she has a new life, somewhere in the Gulf, probably. Maybe north Africa. Either way, her time working as a journalist and sticking her nose into other people's business is well and truly over. And take my word for it, you should walk away from all of this while you still can."

"I'm touched by your concern. Where do I get hold of this Karim Fekir?"

Rüdiger eyed the Beretta. "You go to a club called Le Salon Bleu, in Belleville. He owns it, along with several other businesses."

"You have a picture of him?"

"No, but he's impossible to miss. You could say, he has a weight problem. He's the size of an elephant. Must weigh one hundred and fifty kilos. And he wears a navy-blue fedora hat and most of the time a white three-piece suit. Gold necklace. He sticks out like a *putain* in a nunnery. I have told you all I can. Everything I know. You know what else? I have a little gift for you."

Movement inside the car. He was reaching down into the side pocket. I stepped back, dropped the hammer and raised my gun, firing three rounds through the car door. Loud gunshots, ringing in the ears. Smoke wisps twirling up from the muzzle. The rounds punched neat little holes in the metallic silver steel. Inside the car, Rüdiger jerked and shook, slumping forward and striking his head on the top of the steering wheel. I breathed out and took a step back, raising the gun and aiming at his head. I thought he was probably dead, having taken three rounds in the abdomen. Then he twisted around in his seat and raised a gun. I didn't see what it was. He fired at me through the smashed-out window. His aim was bad and the round ricocheted off the steel rim of the door and disappeared back inside the car. He corrected the aim and fired again. I took cover behind the Berlingo.

Rüdiger kicked open the passenger's door and rolled out onto the concrete floor. He moved fast and with purpose. Not fatally wounded, then. Another roll and he was scrambling to his feet. He ran out of the garage and into the street. I caught the sight of a handgun in his hand glinting in the streetlight as he slipped behind the back of a white Mercedes. He'd had another weapon stashed inside the BMW. No big deal. I had good cover and I waited for something to happen. Turned out I was more patient than he was, and now he darted up from behind the car and rested his hands on the boot and fired a shot at me.

It was high and struck the wall a foot above my head. No

matter, I'd already retreated behind the van the second I saw him bob up into view. He fired again, closer but still a miss. I cradled my gun-hold hand with my left hand and drew in a slow breath. I was behind the truck but had a clear vision of where he was in the BMW's exterior door mirror and I knew what I had to do.

I spun around the end of the truck and swung the gun in a tight arc until I was aiming at his head. Two rounds in the chest and one in the forehead, exploding part of his skull and sending a fine pink mist up into the air where he had been standing until a few seconds ago. Now, he was a crumpled dead heap sprawled out arms and legs akimbo, body on the pavement and legs on the road behind the white Merc. I left the garage and scanned the street but saw no one. Then I walked over to him and took his weapon. Checked it was loaded and slipped it inside the barn coat.

Walking back over to the Peugeot, I saw Michelle looking pale and frozen with fear. Or shock, maybe – I didn't know. I gripped the door handle and swung open the door, sliding down beside her and making the small, old car rock up and down on the shock absorbers for a second or two. It was now I checked the magazine in the Beretta and counted the roads. Then that weapon joined the other gun inside the barn coat, in the opposite pocket.

"My God… You killed him."

Her voice was frail.

"He was trying to kill us, Michelle. If he shot me, you would have been next."

"I know, but still..." She placed a shaking hand on the gear stick and then brought the other hand up to the steering wheel. She checked the mirrors. "What if someone saw us? What if there's a camera somewhere, what if..."

"No one saw and there are no cameras. Not in the immediate vicinity, anyway. It might be wise to lose the car soon anyway, just in case."

"Lose my car? I love this car."

"It's not worth your life."

A long pause. Her right hand came down from the wheel and started to fiddle with the keys hanging from the ignition. "No, I guess not. But I still don't know what just happened."

"You're in shock, that's normal. You just saw a man die. We'll go somewhere quiet and get you a drink and you can take some time to process what just happened. I'll take this forward on my own and then come back and find you when the job is done."

Her eyes were still fixed on the dead man lying behind the Mercedes. "No, please. I don't want to be on my own. Not now."

"Fine, but right now we have to get out of here. Lots of people would have heard those gunshots and called the police. They'll be here in minutes, at best. You want me to drive?"

"No, I know this city better than you. Where do you want me to drive?"

"To Belleville. To the Salon Bleu."

NINE

Belleville is around five kilometres southeast of Montmartre and the drive took twenty minutes. As soon as we arrived, I turned my attention to the property opposite the nightclub Rüdiger had described rather than the club itself. It was a residential building and most of the apartments were occupied. Lights on and people moving around in some of the windows. Next along to the north was also occupied, but the apartment on the other side looked promising. One of the windows was broken and the other was blocked with a graffiti-covered plywood panel. The front door below one of the broken windows was in disrepair with flaking paint and the path was full of weeds breaking up through gaps in between the flagstones. I also noticed that there were no rubbish bins outside the house, unlike the other two on either side of it.

A lucky break.

I told Michelle to hold fast, slammed the car door behind me and stood on the slick pavement. On the other side of the street, I saw a handful of people waiting to get inside the club. They were holding umbrellas and above their heads, a blue and pink neon sign flashed the words *Le Salon Blue* in the drizzle. Instinct drove me to reach down and make sure the Beretta Centurion was all present and correct in my leather barn coat pocket. It was. I prayed the seventeen-round semiautomatic would be enough to handle whatever was inside the club if I had to go in there. For now, I was improvising.

I turned my collar up and approached the club. Halfway towards the queue of people outside the main entrance, I turned right into a narrow alley that looked promising. Large plastic wheelie bins lined the wall on my right and to my left was a low wall running along behind a row of gardens. I turned north onto the Rue des Rigoles intending to make another right turn and head west along the street behind. I counted the houses as I walked and when I was parallel with the one I had already cased and decided was empty, I studied it carefully once again. No obvious sign of habitation from this angle either and the rear was in even worse condition than the front. Like any sprawling metropolis, Paris had its fair share of old, derelict properties and this was just one more example of one of them. A broken marriage maybe, a messy divorce, heavy legal bills, unexpected unemployment, illness, death. Anything could turn a beautiful family home into this mess in a few short months. It was nothing but entropy, the gradual decline of order into chaos.

I wasted no more time and put my money down, smashing the rear gate open with my boot and walking down the path in the centre of the back garden. With a few long, quiet strides I made my way quickly along the path and reached the back door. Wooden with some rot along the base from water splashing up from the step during heavy rain, or maybe from a summer sprinkler set too close to the house. It didn't matter. I was going in through the window to its left, which I now put in with my elbow.

The barn coat's thick leather protected me as I smashed in the pane and then used the Beretta's barrel to sweep the loose shards of glass out of the putty and off the internal windowsill. Job done and I pulled myself in through the window and crashed down with a crunch on the shattered glass all over the interior floor. Gun in hand, I stood still and took stock. As expected, I heard and saw nothing except a quiet, abandoned house. Some cockroaches scattered under the cooker. A moth buzzed against the broken window and finally found its way out. Ahead through the kitchen door, I saw the streetlight from the front of the house glinting on the bannister rail and made my way through to the hall.

My heavy, wet boots pressed down on the wooden stairs and made the steps groan and creak as I held my gun into the aim and made my way up to the top floor. The place did not smell good, and I guessed it was home to more than a few dead rats and mice and probably birds, too, judging by the patina of guano on the landing floor. I looked up to find a hole in the ceiling but had little interest in going as high as the loft. It was unnecessary. I could see everything I needed from the top floor and now made my way into what had once been the master bedroom at the front of the house.

Rotten, moth-eaten curtains draped down either side of the smashed windows and the cold air outside blew what had once been expensive voiles into the room. I waved them out of the way and stepped into the bay window, looking down at the club.

The view was much better from up here, but I was impossible to see from down there. Even sitting outside in a car, I would eventually be clocked, even by an unobservant member of Fekir's security. But from up here, I could monitor them with impunity. If anything near what Michelle had described to me happened to be going on in the club, I now had the perfect viewpoint from which to view it. I turned and saw an old wooden chair beside a bare mattress on the floor. It felt solid so I dragged it over to the window, keeping my gun in my hand. When I was sure the place was safe, I went back around to the car and got Michelle. Any surveillance could last all night, and it would be safer if we were together. When we got back up to the room together, she sat on the side of the bed, on another bare mattress, and looked around with disgust. I doubted someone from her background ever saw anything like this place. But that was her problem. My problem was monitoring the club.

At first, I saw nothing out of the ordinary. Everything was normal. Queues of people lining up outside to get inside out of the rain and have a good night, all very normal. Young men and women dressed in the latest fashions, holding cigarettes at their sides as they laughed and patiently waited to get to know each other better. I gazed along the line until I reached the two men at the door. Bald heads with earpieces and both wearing black suits pulled tight around thick arms. One of them had a tattoo emerging from his suit jacket sleeve. It covered his hand, but I was too far away to see any detail. The apartment above the club was lit but I saw no movement.

"We could be here a long time," I said.

She shrugged. "Whatever it takes to get my sister back."

Whatever it takes, I thought. But exactly how much would it take? I glanced back down at the queue and kept watching for any sign of Karim Fekir because without him, we had no other leads to Juliette. Without Fekir, all of this was for nothing.

TEN

"Have you seen him yet?" Michelle asked. Twenty minutes had passed since we last spoke.

"Not yet. Just the same two meat mountains on the door and a few new punters."

"Maybe Rüdiger was lying. Maybe Fekir isn't a real person at all and all of this is just a waste of time while they take Juliette further away from me."

After checking no one was approaching the club, I turned away momentarily from the street and looked at her. "Don't talk like that. Try and stay positive. Besides, I have a feeling Rüdiger was being truthful."

"How can you be so sure?"

I recalled him begging not to die, muzzle pressed up against his temple. I shrugged. "Just a hunch."

Her shadow fell to one side, a black silhouette in a square of yellow plaster, lit by the flashing neon of the club opposite. She lit a cigarette and tipped her head back against the wall. I watched the smoke's pale shadow twisting up to the ceiling. Our chances of finding Juliette were hanging by a thread.

"You think we'll ever see her again?" she asked.

"We'll do everything we can."

"This is not what I asked, Bill."

I closed my eyes and tipped my head back, feeling the cold wall on my head. She both deserved the truth and did not deserve it, at the same time.

"Maybe, Michelle. I wish I could say yes."

Music from the club pulsed out into the street. The queue grew longer.

"How long have you been on the road?" she asked.

"A few days, more or less."

"You're on the run, aren't you?"

I smiled. "I'm just looking for somewhere to hang my hat, that's all. But enough about me."

"Enough about you! I barely know the first thing about you."

Outside the club, an argument broke out. I turned and saw the two doormen pushing a young man in a leather jacket out of the way to allow a fat, older man into the club ahead of him.

"What do you make of this?" I asked.

Michelle got up and walked over to the window. Carefully, she pulled back the filthy voiles and watched the action down on the pavement outside Le Salon Bleu. "Someone seems to have a VIP pass to get into the club ahead of the line," she said. "You think this is Fekir?"

I did. He matched the description given to me by Rüdiger back in Montmartre almost perfectly. Fedora, white suite, necklace. This guy was a walking avatar. I couldn't make out the colour of the hat in the darkness. Rüdiger had said navy blue, but this just looked black. "It looks like him to me. Rüdiger told me Fekir was a Moroccan man in the habit of wearing fedoras and was at least one hundred and fifty kilos. He also said he owned Le Salon Bleu. I think right now we can safely assume that guy is Fekir. Whore in a nunnery is about right, though given what I know about him, I'd say he sticks out more like a turd in a punch bowl."

"Bill?"

"Sorry, just thinking out loud. Passes the time."

"But that's him, the one in that terrible suit? That's the man who kidnapped my sister?"

"If Rüdiger was telling the truth, then yes. He's one of the circle involved in her kidnapping. And he's the man who ordered Rüdiger to get Manu Badeaux to put the frighteners on you. We'll get more information when we have a talk to him about it."

"If it is him, and he took her, I will kill him, Bill. I swear it."

"That's easy to say, Michelle, but another thing to do. Taking someone's life takes a few seconds but you carry it in your soul forever."

She thought about that for a few seconds. Right now, her rage could propel her to the edge of taking someone's life, but dropping off the edge was a much bigger step. At least it was the first time. But she was defiant. I saw it in her eyes. "If he has killed her, that is a price I am willing to pay. Bastard."

Still, I guessed she was all talk. I'd heard it before, and who could blame her. Her baby sister was missing, maybe dead, all because of Fekir and his associates. I know what the punishment would be if they'd done it to someone in my family but it would do no good to talk like this in front of Michelle. I had to put the fire in her heart out, not fan the flames. Outside, Fekir had now gone into the club and one of the doormen was reading the riot act to the teenager who had kicked up.

I said, "Let's just take it easy and try and get to the bottom of things first. The only thing that's important right now is getting Juliette back. When she's safe, we can talk about settling the account with Fekir and his little trafficking circle."

"It's not little," she said. "It goes right to the top. Higher than that creature down there. If we save Juliette, we'll all have to change our names and start new lives somewhere far away. They will never stop hunting us."

"I won't let that happen."

She laughed, turning away from the window and

slumping down in the old wooden chair I had been sitting on. "I don't want to disrespect you, Bill. Not after all you have done for me, but what can you do? You are one man. We're talking about an organized group of people traffickers with connections to the very top of government. They will snuff you out like a candle." She began to sob. "They will kill us all. What are we doing here? I should just accept Juliette is gone and walk away."

"We're not walking anywhere, but Fekir is."

She looked up at me. "He's already leaving the club?"

"Looks like it. And now he has a nice package under his arm, too. Maybe it's payday."

She was up out of the chair and looking through the voiles again. "He'll get payback all right."

I checked my weapon was loaded and ready to use, then pushed it back into my pocket. "First, the facts. Michelle. Always the facts. When the stakes are this high, we use caution in the extreme, then, if we get the right person, we terminate with extreme prejudice. Always in that order."

She thought about that, too. "So, what do we do now?"

Outside, a long, black Mercedes was gliding to a stop outside the club. The driver hopped out and ran around to the rear door, which he opened with a flourish. Fekir squeezed inside and the driver shut the door. He returned to his seat and turned the engine on.

"We follow that car. Let's get down to your car and get

going before we lose him."

Unexpectedly, Michelle kissed me on the cheek, leaving a pale circle of lipstick on my face and the scent of her perfume lingering around me. She did this because she had felt a surge of hope. She thought we were going to get her sister back. She moved away from me and walked over to the bed and picked up her bag from the mattress. "Thank you for this. For all you are doing. Do you think this is the break we're looking for?"

I thought about the best answer. Not fair to build up her confidence in case her sister was already dead, or maybe just impossible to find. On the other hand, she needed something to hold onto with both hands, something to keep her morale up.

"We're doing everything we can to find Juliette and right now that means following Fekir. Time to roll."

ELEVEN

Back out on the streets and we were three cars behind the Merc limo, radio on low and wipers sweeping light rain from the windscreen. The Peugeot's cheap cloth seats were worn down, broken and uncomfortable. This became more obvious the longer I spent sitting in them. Fekir was heading southwest, but that was all I knew. Occasionally his driver weaved through the traffic and disappeared in front of a truck and they became partially obscured. One lucky break was his car. It was the only Mercedes limousine I had seen all night, so keeping an eye on it was that much easier.

"What do you think was in the package he got in the club?" Michelle asked.

"Cash or drugs, most likely. I'd go with cash."

"Why?"

"Easier to explain if you're caught with it. Think about it. He was waving it around all over the place like a flag. I doubt even a man like Fekir would be wafting several kilos of illegal narcotics around like that. Money. It was money, almost certainly connected to the trafficking operation."

"Give me half a chance and I'll burn every single note of it."

Burning the cash was an improvement on wanting to kill Fekir, and I was about to respond to her when my phone rang. I pulled it from the barn coat and answered. "Blake."

"Bonsoir, Colonel."

I didn't recognize the voice. Despite the use of French, I had heard the controlled, icy tones of the upper-class Englishman.

"Who is this?"

"You can call me Sparrowhawk."

I took a second out to think about this. Checked my speed and the rear-view mirrors to make sure we weren't being followed. I'd had calls like this before. Calls out of nowhere made by people I didn't know. People with a distinct advantage over me. "Your parents didn't like you very much, did they?"

"You still have a sense of humour, Colonel Blake. This is good."

"I won't ask you how or where you got my number."

"That would probably be best."

"But because I'm a busy man with a lot to do, I will ask why am I speaking to you, Sparrowhawk?"

A long pause. "Because we need to talk. Naturally."

Michelle was staring at me. My eyes were on the limo ahead, but I could feel hers crawling all over me. I pushed the phone down into my chest to block the receiver. "It's fine. An old friend."

She looked sceptical but said nothing. Lit a cigarette in the darkness.

"You smoke too much," I said with a smile. Then, I returned to the call. "You say we need to talk, Sparrowhawk. Tell me, is this a mutually beneficial arrangement or are you on the scrounge?"

He gave a brief, subdued laugh. "Mutually beneficial, to a certain degree."

After deciding it didn't matter if Michelle overheard the call or not, I set the phone to speaker and propped it in the little mobile phone holder she'd set up next to her steering wheel. "And to what degree would that be?"

"Let's just say that right now, you need me more than I need you, but that will change in the future."

"So this is an investment for you."

"You could put it that way."

Seeing the Merc signal right and turn onto another boulevard, I did the same thing but retained the distance between us. It was not possible to tell if they had seen us or not. In the movies, the pursued car realises and takes off at speed and a chase ensues. In reality, if they figure out they're being followed, they're more likely to call up some extra backup, lead you somewhere dangerous, block you in and go about you mob-handed. This is not what Michelle and I needed tonight. With this in mind, and cruising smoothly on the new road, I replied to Sparrowhawk.

"I think it's time you got to the point."

He said, "Very well. You're in trouble. Big trouble."

Only one thing came to mind. The obvious thing. "Is this about Wildhorse?"

Wildhorse was a covert operation deep inside the British Foreign and Commonwealth Office, run at the time by the Foreign Secretary Sir Michael Mulgrave. It involved certain radical elements in the FCO identifying terror threats and then deliberately letting them go ahead on British soil in order to foment a violent public reaction. This was required to manipulate police direction. I brought the whole thing down in less than twenty-four hours.

Sparrowhawk's voice hardened. "Yes. Wildhorse."

"Quartermain, then."

Another pause, this time I detected anger in his voice. "Right again. Quartermain."

Jack Quartermain was an ex-bootneck, a Royal Marine Commando. I'd worked with him on missions in the past. An odd figure. A loner. Hard. Unapproachable and very dangerous. These days, he works as an assassin for the nasty end of Her Majesty's Government. When I took down Wildhorse, Sir Michael Mulgrave activated a kill order on me, codename *Taipan*. Turned out, Quartermain was the man for the job.

"Are you in D19?" I asked.

"D19 was officially stood down after the Mulgrave scandal. You know that."

The Merc slowed and took another turn, this time right. I followed it across a wide junction and into a labyrinthine quarter of the city. "I've always been more interested in the unofficial side of life."

Another long pause and a sigh. "All operations previously included in the D19 brief have been transferred to another unnamed division. It's still casually called D19 by old-timers."

I almost smiled. "That sounds about right."

"You're an old hand, Colonel. You know how these things work."

"Unfortunately, yes. I take it Quartermain is all charged up and on the loose."

"He's on his way to Paris. He left RAF Northolt on board a military jet an hour ago. He's coming to pay you a visit and see to it you never leave the City of Light, unless you're in a box, that is."

An hour ago. If Sparrowhawk was telling the truth, Quartermain was almost certainly on one of the BAe 146 short-haul jets commonly requisitioned by D19. Accounting for air traffic control in Paris and possible stacking, I guessed he would be touching down around now. "How kind of him to pay me a visit."

"He means business, Blake. He was in pretty tight with Mulgrave and Shepherd and the rest of the team and played a key role in Wildhorse. If you hadn't already worked it out, his were some of the fingerprints on the bombs in London, Luton and Liverpool. I mean that literally. He's a very versatile operative."

"I know Quartermain."

"Then you'll know how determined he is to see out his mission. When Mulgrave sent him the codeword *Taipan* he signed your death warrant. Quartermain will not stop until Operation Taipan is completed, and that means taking you permanently out of the equation."

I kept an eye on the Mercedes limo, still cruising through the Paris rain. Michelle pushed her window down an inch. She was reaching the end of her smoke. I checked our speed. No sense in getting pulled for speeding at a time like this.

"Quartermain has to do what he has to do. If he's flying out to Paris to track me down, then so be it. He has to find me first, anyway. It's a big city. It could take him days, by which time I'll be long gone. Unless of course, you're planning on giving him a helping hand."

A dark laugh. "So suspicious."

"If you are, you can forget it. Even with a track on the phone, I'll be out of this location in minutes. I'll dump the phone."

"I'm not here to help Quartermain track you down,

Blake. I'm here to help you evade him."

"Why?"

"Because I want you to live. I strongly suggest for this reason that you do not dump the phone. It's the only way I can communicate with you. Take my word for it, it's in your interest."

"But I don't trust you."

"I'd be disappointed in you if you did."

"Then what next, Sparrowhawk?"

"What next, is that I have a little surprise for you. Are sitting comfortably?"

TWELVE

"I'm sitting just fine thanks," I replied. "What's your little surprise?"

"Quartermain doesn't know it yet, but I'm tracking him."

"Interesting."

"He'll work it out eventually, naturally, but until he does you now have an advantage."

"As I said, he has to find me first."

"Operation Taipan is unofficially sanctioned by HMG, Blake. Quartermain has access to all British SIS data and intel, plus the French are on board, as are Interpol and Europol. You can guarantee they already know everything. Where you entered France, where you're staying, maybe even the nutritional content of your last meal. CCTV data and passport intel. Everything."

Most French hotels required a passport to be presented to check-in. This goes for hotels all over Europe. It's a fundamental difference in freedom compared with checking into hotels in most English-speaking countries. This is why

I planned to ask Michelle to use her passport if we had to check into a hotel any time tonight. At this time, she was still safe, but if what Sparrowhawk said was true, it wouldn't take the roving eye of the international intel apparatus long to link her to me. She was already way out of her depth and she didn't even know it yet.

"I'm not travelling on my own passport, Sparrowhawk. I was there that night, on the roof of Mulgrave's mansion when he set Quartermain on me. I'm not a fool."

"No one said you were, but my advice is you should get out of Paris. Now."

"I can handle Quartermain."

"Many a good man has said that. He's our most dangerous assassin, Blake. You know that."

Sparrowhawk was right. I was a heavily trained and experienced D19 operative, but Quartermain was in a league all of his own. Everyone in the division knew it. Very little was known about his personal life. Tough London childhood in the East End. Royal Marine Commando at sixteen. Special Boat Service operative in his late twenties. Serious involvement in special ops in Afghanistan, Iraq, Sierra Leone and other places that are seriously off the books, like Ukraine, Belarus and the South China Sea. He was respected but a loner. Perfect material for D19 covert ops. I could see why they'd sent him after me. Set a thief to catch a thief.

"You said that Operation Taipan is unofficially sanctioned by HMG," I said. "Does this mean Firebrace is on board with it?"

He hesitated a full three seconds. Matthew Firebrace was the new British Foreign Secretary and would be in a small circle of officials and family members who knew exactly what had happened to his predecessor, Sir Michael Mulgrave. The official line reported to the public was that he had died in a tragic suicide, but the reality was different. I had shot Mulgrave in the chest and blown him off his own roof. Whether he had died on impact with the ground or from the bullet in his heart, it was hard to say. Either way, governments tended to frown on this sort of thing, despite rumours Firebrace was on the right side and vehemently opposed what Mulgrave had tried to. But you didn't stake your life on rumours.

"As far as I know, the new Foreign Secretary does not know about Taipan."

"That's a shame. Why doesn't someone like you tell him?"

"Perhaps you overestimate my reach."

After a long pause, I said, "Why are you telling me this?"

"Let's just say I am not an unbridled fan of the old regime, which still exists in certain quarters. And besides, one hand washes the other, Blake. I help you now and you help me later."

"You seem pretty certain of that."

"You need my help tonight, Colonel. Take my word for that. Think about what I have just told you and if you survive Quartermain, we'll talk later."

He cut the call.

Michelle broke the silence. "He doesn't sound like a friend."

I put the phone in my pocket. "Friend might have been a slight exaggeration. Let's say a work colleague."

"And what is work? You still haven't told me."

"No, I haven't."

"You said you were a retired soldier, but not what you do now."

I ignored her. Up ahead, the Merc was slowing in the rain and pulling over to the pavement. I said, "Heads up, it looks like Fekir wants a bite to eat. He's pulling up outside some kind of restaurant. You ever heard of Chez Karim?"

She shook her head. "I never come to this part of the city."

"It's just speculation, but it must be his place. His name is Karim Fekir, after all."

I pulled up on the pavement and we watched the driver perform the same ritual in reverse. He climbed out of the car, only this time he popped open an umbrella as he ran around to the rear door. Then he opened the car and shielded Fekir from the rain, walking the big man over to the restaurant. He was still holding the package. When Fekir was inside, the driver folded the umbrella down and returned to the car. The rear lights lit up red in the night and then he drove away, joining the traffic and turning out of sight at the end of the road.

"We can pull up in there," she said, pointing to a small car park opposite the restaurant.

I pulled the Peugeot off the road and into a car park at the side of the restaurant. The headlights swept across a black-painted cinderblock wall as the car steered in a tight arc and swung into a parking space beside a large, rusted skip covered in graffiti. I cut the engine and stepped out into the cold night. A sharp wind cut through the car park and rainclouds skidded across the sky above the club, low and dark.

I leaned into the open door. "Stay here."

THIRTEEN

I turned away and walked around to the front of the restaurant, Beretta Centurion in my pocket. Collar up, hands in pockets and eyes to the ground, I took in as much as I could in my peripheral vision. The wind blew again, picking up litter and skimming it along the pavement. It was cold and stung my lips and eyes.

After noting a few CCTV cameras, I walked over to Chez Karim's front window. Inside was a small reception area with a desk covered in laminated menus and fake pot plants. There was a laptop and an open notebook with a pen on it but no sign of the maître d'. I could see some of the main dining area behind the desk, now around half full of happy diners. Warm tables lit with little flickering tea lights, others had candles protruding from wax-coated wine bottles. Inside, the air hummed with small talk, but not out here on the pavement. Out here was cold and dark. Someone coughed as they walked past me, head tucked down into his scarf.

I opened the door and stepped into the reception. The

scent of Middle Eastern spices hung in the air like a mist. Still no maître d', so I spun the book around and ran my finger down a list of names. All neat and up to date. I guessed their computer had screwed up so many times they used the book as a backup. A good idea. Then I found the name I was looking for, Fekir, with a female guest, seated at table nine. Even the boss got checked in. That was all right with me. I spun the book to its original place and walked around the desk. Still no maitre d'. I wondered where he could be because it wasn't in here. Most likely the kitchen. There were only three places he could be, after all. The other was the gents.

I stepped out into the main dining room, scanning the little table number holders as I went and immediately drawing some attention. I'm a tall guy and I was on my own and wearing a barn coat dripping with rain. I looked out of place and people always notice unusual things. It's a mechanism of evolution, but I didn't let it get to me. It wasn't personal. I found table nine over against the far wall. It was the best table in the house. I saw Fekir sitting with his back to me, opposite a woman with dark hair and lots of makeup. She was dressed to the nines for her big night out with one of France's biggest people traffickers. I wondered if she knew that as I brushed past a young couple eating salmon en papillote at table seven. They also turned to look at me.

There is a biological phenomenon called gaze detection. This is a sensitive neurological response that alerts people to the gaze of others. If they see you looking at them in their peripheral vision, the response causes them to break away from what they are doing and look right back. This is what happened right now with the woman sitting opposite Fekir. She looked up from her plate of food and stared right at me, just as I was bearing down on them. Fekir now looked up at her and spoke. He was asking what she was looking at, and without waiting for a response, he now hooked his arm behind the back of his chair for leverage and twisted his fat body around to see what was going on.

I had already arrived at the table.

"Are you Karim Fekir?" I asked.

The fat man said, "Who are you?"

"Rüdiger said you had a weight problem but I think he was being polite."

His face changed. He dabbed at some sauce on his mouth and threw the napkin down on the table beside the bouillabaisse. "How dare you come in here and talk to me like this. Who are you?"

"I asked you first. Are you Karim Fekir?"

His eyes told me what his mouth wanted to keep secret.

"I thought so. Here's the problem I have, Karim. I need to talk to you about the massive people trafficking operation you help to run, but I'm wondering if this is the right place.

Just thinking about your reputation as a restaurateur, that's all."

"What is this, Karim?" the woman asked, horrified.

Fekir blew out a breath and took in another one. The twisted position he was sitting in was crushing his substantial body fat up against his diaphragm. "You think you can come in here and insult me with these lies?"

He was blustering, compounding the trouble he was in. It fell on deaf ears.

"One of the women you recently kidnapped was named Juliette Dupont. I want to know where she is, and I want to know right now."

He turned in the chair, which squeaked under his weight. I saw his kneecaps flex under his suit trousers. This signalled to me he was putting pressure on them and getting ready to stand up. He hefted his considerable bulk out of the wooden seat and turned to face me. The big man who owned Chez Karim clearly wasn't about to be insulted and humiliated in his own backyard. He had to teach me a lesson. He actually smiled at me, dipped his head down and lowered his voice to a whisper. A few words between old friends.

"You know who I am?" he said.

"God, please," the woman said. "Not here, Karim. Not again."

I noticed movement in the kitchen, behind the traffic doors. Two men, probably his bodyguards. "No. I don't know who you are. Why not tell me, Karim?"

He nodded his head and smiled more. He already knew what to do with me. His mind was made up. He had decided to take out the trash. "Let me tell you who I am. I'm not the sort of man you accuse of doing things like you just said in here. Not at all. You know what happened to the last guy who talked to me like that?"

I looked at my watch. "I don't care about him. I won't ask again, Fekir. Where is Juliette Dupont?"

He shook his head and lifted his hand to place it on my shoulder. Straight-forward body language to assert his dominance. "Now, hear me when I speak to you. I will only say this one time."

I rotated my upper body and took hold of the fat hand, twisting it at the wrist and folding it back until the back of his hand was pressing down on the flesh of his forearm. The bones snapped and he screamed, pulling the hand from my grip, tears already flooding from his eyes.

The woman screamed. People dining at nearby tables rose from their chairs, stunned and staring, waiting for anyone else to make the next move. The two guys I'd seen lingering in the kitchen had been keeping an eye on the boss through the little windows, occasionally wiping the kitchen steam away. Now, they burst through the traffic doors and made their way over to me. The one in the lead top-vaulted over the countertop. The guy behind him, older-looking who seemed kind of bored, raised his eyes to heaven and took a second to open the countertop door. It was time to move things along, so I exerted some more pressure on Fekir's wrist and forced him down onto his knees. When he was down and out, I released his wrist and waited for the two bodyguards to catch up with us and get over to the table.

I wondered if maybe I was starting to get somewhere.

FOURTEEN

Down on his knees, Fekir was still staring at his red, swollen hand and screaming. He had been supporting the hand with the shattered wrist by cradling it up against his chest. When he let go to see what would happen, the hand flopped around like it was made of rubber. He wailed and took it up again, cradling it once more against his chest. The two guys from the kitchen finally arrived at the table.

"A sparkling water, thanks," I said to the first guy.

He reached inside his jacket. It wasn't for sparkling water. I grabbed the back of Fekir's now empty chair and swung it against the guy's head. When it impacted against his skull, the chair broke up like in some old Western movie, but the job was done. It knocked him out and he crashed down onto the carpet beside Fekir's table. Something bordering chaos now broke out in the restaurant. Everyone who had been eating and enjoying their evening and who was not already standing up was now up and out of their chairs. Some of the tougher-looking guys had kept hold of their dinner knives and were trying to stand their ground, saving face in front of their wives and girlfriends, but most of the men were now being dragged out of the room by their better halves. I knew each one of them would be on the phone to the law the second they thought they were safe.

The second man from the kitchen had taken a step back but now drew a knife. It was a simple switchblade, and he was holding it all wrong. He was also waiting for me to go to him. He threw it from one hand to the other and beckoned me to step forward. The theatrics told me all I needed to know. I lunged towards him, easily smacking the blade from his hand, rotated in a half-circle and jabbed my right elbow into his windpipe. His eyes widened like saucers as he struggled for breath. Gasping like a fish out of water, I decked him with a left-hook and he crashed back on the table behind him, smashing bowls of soup and baskets of garlic bread all over the place. I turned my attention back to Fekir.

"Juliette's location, Karim. Now, or I'll burn this bastard place down with you in it."

The big man from Morocco made little attempt to hide his fear, which I respected. His dark eyes crawled over the two unconscious bodies of his close protection, then he looked at me.

"There is a house in Barbès-Rochechouart. It's a sort of safehouse run by the operation. A lot of men stay there. A man named Amzazi keeps some of the women there sometimes until things have cooled down. Last time I heard, the Dupont girl was there."

"You have the address on your phone?" I asked.

He nodded.

"Find it, now."

He reached into his pocket with his good hand and found the contacts list. He showed it to me. I took the phone out of his hand and scrolled down until I had seen the whole list. "I see no Amzazi."

He looked confused. "It should be in there."

"It's not. So, write it down the old-fashioned way. Fast."

I pulled one of the napkins from the table and pushed it in front of him. He paused, then reached into his suit pocket with his good hand and drew the pen out. "I cannot write. You have crushed my writing hand."

"Give me the pen and tell me."

He handed it to me. It was heavy in my hand, an eighteen-carat gold plate etched with art nouveau flowers and what looked like a classic Montblanc diamond on the cap. Nice, but extravagant and drifting towards the tasteless. I wrote down the address as he told me it.

"If this is a wild goose chase, I'll be at your home address before sunrise. You, your family, anyone, I don't care. If you're lying, someone will pay. You'll all pay."

He said, "It's the right address. Please, don't tell the men you find there who gave it to you."

"I make no promises."

I kicked him in the face and knocked him out. His heavy body flopped back onto the carpet, reminding me of a dead seal. On his phone, I signed out of several GPS tracking apps and his Gmail and iCloud accounts and pocketed it and then told the woman he had been dining with to call him an ambulance. Then I left Chez Karim and set off in the rain back to the car. It was still cold and wet but the old barn coat protected me from the weather well. It did a good job. Collar up and chin tucked down inside the front, rain at my back, it was almost like being in my front room. Almost. Of course, I guessed someone at Chez Karim might be following me on the CCTV cameras I had clocked outside the restaurant on my way in. Not a bad surveillance system, but I made sure to stay inside its field of vision and avoid the obvious blind spots. No sense in letting them think I was afraid of them.

I rounded the side of the restaurant and wandered back down to the car park. Looking through the rain I gazed over at the lost woman sitting in the old, used Peugeot. It would still have been possible to walk away, to give her the address and let her hire another private investigator, but something told me to stay on it and help her find the missing woman. On the surface, it was the right thing to do, but Quartermain was throwing a spanner in the works. Now, I had to keep one eye on Juliette's kidnapping and another on the killer who was tracking me down. But then, Quartermain would be on my trail whether or not I helped Michelle find her sister so I decided to stay with her to the end.

I approached the Peugeot but did not attempt to catch Michelle's attention. She was now slumped down in the driver's seat almost out of sight with a newspaper obscuring her face. As I drew closer to the car, I heard a drunk cry out in the night. A taxi splashed in some puddles forming on the stone-laid gutters. Streetlights burned in the drizzle. It was dark and it was cold. Sensible people were in bed, warm and safe.

Inside the car, I said, "I'm going to need something a little more substantial than this Beretta."

"What do you mean?" She sat up, her eyes full of hope. "You know where she is?"

"Maybe. But I'm not tackling a safehouse full of North African people traffickers with a nine-mil handgun. I need something a little more persuasive. Some chunkier hardware."

"But from where? You cannot just buy weapons like this in Paris. There are licenses and permits and…"

"We're not going to a shop, Michelle."

"Then where, at this time of night?"

"We're going to see an old friend of mine. C'mon, turn the ignition and let's get out of here. It's late and time's running out."

FIFTEEN

There wasn't much talk between us during the drive over to Bonzo Butler's place. I kept thinking that she wanted me to say something just to break the silence, but I never did. Instead, I listened to the engine. It was a small 1.4-litre petrol with a low, dull knocking sound coming from maybe the cylinder head or the engine block. Could be a problem with the crankshaft or the connecting rods. It was not long for this world but I saw from the mileage it had more than done its job. I guessed it could hang on another few hours and see me through the night.

Later, when we pulled up near Bonzo's house and locked the car, we walked down to the place he'd told me about on the phone when I'd called him to see if he was in. He was in Paris, but not at home and he suggested we wait for him to return at one of his favourite places, the Café de la Paix. They called it a café, but in truth it was just a small, forgotten bar somewhere few tourists ever wandered, hidden away behind a rain-streaked window distorting the warm lights inside. Michelle had also made a call in the car, contacting an old friend she thought might help us. She had arranged to meet him here, too. Now, she peered through the window trying to find him, but no such luck.

We stepped into the place and no one turned to look at us. There was a short, polished wooden bar. On one side, a tired man in a grey suit reached up to his collar and loosened his necktie before downing a shot of whisky. On the other side, opposite him, a fat man with long hair and a handlebar moustache was taking glasses out of a dishwasher in a cloud of steam and stacking them in a neat line on a chrome overbar glass rack. He wore a black waistcoat over a red shirt.

"I need a drink." Michelle brushed past me and headed over to the bar. She caught the barman's eye and ordered two Stella Artois beers. He cracked open the bottles and poured them into two stem glasses with the smooth deft touch of a man existing somewhere between the well-experienced and the weary. He slid them over to us and told her how much they cost and she went to pay on her card. I stopped her and handed her a twenty euro note. No tracks, no trace. She passed it to him with a polite smile.

"Enjoy," he said, already finding the next customer out of the corner of his eye.

"Keep the change."

"Merci."

We walked over to the back of the bar and sat on two rattan bistro chairs. The tired man at the bar ordered another whisky. Behind him, another man read a newspaper. At the front of the bar, a young couple were speaking quietly and sipping *noisettes* from small china cups branded with the café's name. Gentle cocktail jazz piano drifted in the air alongside the scent of the coffee and the whisky. A police car flashed past in the street outside, splashing arcs of gutter water into the air and strobing the café's interior with neon blue lights. Then it was gone.

"It's fine," I said. "They're not after us."

Michelle was still looking over her shoulder at the street outside. "Maybe not, or maybe they are. I don't think I'll ever be able to sleep again, or even relax."

"Are you hungry? We have some time to kill before Bonzo is ready to see us."

She picked up the menu and nodded. We ordered some food and waited for it to come. People came and went. Then the food arrived. We ate gougères. No drinks. She poked at the little cheese puffs with a distinct lack of interest, eyeing instead her packet of cigarettes beside the greasy plate. The No Smoking sign on the table wasn't joking anymore. In Paris, the smoker gets a €450 fine and the guy behind the bar has to find €750. That's the incentive to wait until you're done with your meal.

I finished eating and ordered another Stella. "Earlier, you mentioned the police did nothing when you called them about your sister. You want to go into a little more detail about that?"

"It is just as I say. Because they are in on it!" she said. "Juliette told me. That is what she was investigating, Bill. Young women being kidnapped and abused by high-profile clients not just in France but across all of Europe. That is why they took her! To silence her. God knows what they're putting her through."

"You don't know the police won't do anything. It's a big organization. They can't all be working with the traffickers. Maybe there's a chance someone can help after all. I mean if things don't work out tonight." Not that I wanted to spell it out, but I was thinking about what happened if they got Juliette out of the country. After that, I could no longer help and she would need to look elsewhere.

But in response to my question, she had hesitated before replying. She took a sip of beer and I could see something was on her mind. Eventually, she answered me. "Yes, I do know they will be of no help. I know very well. Bill, there is something I did not tell you."

SIXTEEN

She sighed and looked down at her drink. Took another long sip. "A long time ago, I worked in the police."

I sipped the beer, controlled my reaction. "Go on."

"It's not important, and has no bearing on our search for my sister or I would have told you. But, a few years ago I was in the Paris Police Prefecture working as a detective. At first, I did well and was promoted, but then I started working on some cold cases. Some murders, but mostly missing women from all over France. I became obsessed with finding them."

"I can imagine."

"Going through their files every day for months had a serious effect on me. When I closed my eyes at night I saw their faces looking back at me. I am not a naïve person, but I had no idea how bad this world could be until I started in that job. Young women taken in the night, just snatched off the streets on their way home. Taken from bus stops and taxi ranks, never to see their loved ones again. Drugged in clubs and bars and dragged away. It became too much."

"So you quit?"

She shook her head, almost imperceptibly. "No."

"Then, what happened?"

"There was one girl, in particular, I wanted to find more than any of the others. I had no idea who she was. It was just something about her eyes. The way she looked at me from the photographs. Her parents had died in a car crash in Italy years earlier, and she was raised by her grandmother. The old woman was still alive, crushed by the disappearance of her only grandchild. I swore that if she was alive, I would find her and bring her home."

"But that never worked out, did it?"

"No. I started looking into the case more and more. Scratching deeper under the surface. The girl's name was Audrey Bourgoin. She came from Chartres but moved to Paris when she was eighteen to study at the Sorbonne. She was here less than six months when she vanished."

"Circumstances?"

"Walking home from a party in Val-de-Grâce. Witnesses said she left them at midnight and her apartment was less than twenty minutes away. Her roommate said she never made it. Police looked into it but found nothing. No sign of murder. No body. Her family was poor, but still, there was no ransom note, anyway. Nothing. She just vanished into thin air."

"When was this?"

"Ten years ago. I started on the cold cases around a year

after her disappearance, nine years ago."

"I'm guessing you found a trail someone didn't want you to find."

She nodded, eyes flicking down to the table. "Unfortunately, this is what happened. My enquiries led me to a car seen at the scene of her disappearance. When I checked up on it, I found the car was registered to a man named Nicolas Duris."

"The name rings a bell."

"It should. He is the EU Commissioner for Trade."

"That's right. I remember."

"He is best known for a corrupt investment deal with the Chinese Communist Party. Somehow he got away with it. Friends in high places, I guess, but it should have brought him down. Let's just say he will soon be retiring in style."

I nodded, recalling a news clip I had seen of Nicolas Duris and Sir Michael Mulgrave, the former British Foreign Secretary, holding a grip and grin session for the world's press over some kind of trade treaty a few years ago. Talk about keeping bad company. I decided not to tell Michelle about my brief association with Mulgrave and move back to her story.

"What happened next?"

"Then I was framed for stealing money we seized from a bank raid and thrown out of the force, no appeal and no pension. I told Juliette what had happened and I think that is where she got the idea to go after them, but from a different angle."

"From the journalist point of view?"

She gave a quick nod. "Oui. You see now why I blame myself."

I was about to reply when the man she had called on the drive over entered the café with a glance over his shoulder. He recognized her at once and stepped over, pausing at the bar to order a beer of his own. I watched him wait for his beer. Short, well-built. Brown hair, cropped right down. Hadn't shaved. Clothes looked expensive but old and tired. He walked over to our table with purpose, taking care to check behind out in the street one more time before joining us at the table.

He kissed Michelle on both cheeks then nodded at me. "Bonsoir."

Michelle smiled thinly. "Bill, this is the old friend of mine I told you about. His name is Gabriel Laurent. He was a cop, too."

I took a cigarette from Michelle's packet and pulled some matches from my pocket. "I thought you didn't trust cops these days."

"This was a long time ago," Laurent said, pulling up a chair. "Back before the corruption of the old regime. I left that behind me, but maybe I can help today."

Michelle gave him a wan smile and let her eyes drop away

to the drink in front of her. "I hope so."

After a pause, he said, "Michelle, perhaps we could talk outside."

"I have no secrets from Bill," she said. "He has risked his life to save me and my sister."

He looked at me awkwardly. "Nevertheless..."

"It's fine," I said to her. "You go. I'll wait here and maybe drink another beer."

SEVENTEEN

Michelle and Laurent talked outside, standing just out of the rain under the café's awning. Something about the guy bothered me, but I couldn't work out what that might be. Back in the day, we'd have called him shifty. I finished the beer and then ordered two coffees. I had to stay sharp. Under the circumstances, Michelle was holding up better than most would, but she was starting to fray around the edges. I'd already seen some of the signs. Fiddling with her hands more. Tapping her leg under the table. Drifting away into headspace and not following the conversation.

My phone rang.

I picked it up and saw a number I didn't recognize. I thought maybe it was Sparrowhawk, but I was wrong. I answered the call.

"Who's speaking?" I said.

"That's not polite."

"I don't like cold calls."

"Then I'll come to the point. You're working with the Dupont woman. Looking for her sister."

He was speaking English, but no French accent. The accent was Arabic. North African. I recognized the cadence and placed it in Morocco. I doubted it was Fekir who had put them onto me because he seemed so keen on their not knowing he had squealed on them. Then again, maybe he had tried to curry favour by warning them and letting them get out in front of me. None of this mattered. What mattered was who they were and what they wanted. "Who is this?"

"This is a warning. You back off now or both of those women are dead. We're watching you all the time, Blake."

It wasn't great finding out that they knew my name but I kept my voice low and measured. "I feel at a disadvantage. You know my name but I don't know yours."

"And that is how it stays."

"We'll see about that."

He laughed. "Listen to me, Colonel Blake. Listen to me carefully." His voice grew harder. "Are you listening to me very carefully?"

"Say your piece."

"You go home now, back to London. If you stay on our trail, I will kill the Dupont women, like I just said to you, a second ago." I heard him sucking on a cigarette or cigar. The receiver crackled as he blew smoke into the speaker. I kept my mouth shut and checked my watch. Outside, Michelle and Laurent were starting to argue. Arms raised, pointing.

Raised voices. She clasped her head in her hands and turned around in despair, stepping out into the rain. Laurent placed his arm on her shoulder and wheeled her back under the awning again. After a long pause, I said, "Tell me, is Juliette Dupont safe?"

"You know it in your heart. Why else would you be trying to find her? You do all this to give Michelle Dupont the corpse of her sister? Besides, what do you care if she is safe or not? Go home. Take your pension. Leave us alone. You have no idea who you are screwing around with, friend."

The idea of going home was a non-starter. I wasn't sure I could even get back into the United Kingdom without the authorities arresting me at the border. I had no intention of going back anyway. "Is she safe?"

There was another long pause, men mumbling in Arabic. I had been right. The dialect was Moroccan, very hard to understand. I had some basic training in Gulf Arabic, and a little more in Masri, the dialect spoken in Egypt. The latter was the easiest to understand. Moroccan was the hardest, so I caught only a few words. *Girl, telephone, gag.* After another few seconds, I heard a young woman's voice. She spoke in French, desperate and scared. "Mimi, c'est toi?"

"It's not Michelle," I said in French. "Listen carefully, Juliette. I'm working with your sister to find you. If you can tell me anything about where you —."

"Tsk, tsk, Colonel Blake," said the man's voice. "That

was very naughty of you."

"Let her go, now. I give you my word, you will regret it if you don't."

The voice grew hotter, raised. "You do not threaten me, Colonel! You are nothing. You are a little man trying to break into a big machine. You do not win this fight. End your pursuit, or not only will both of these women die, but so will you. After all, what you did to Karim Fekir was not polite. You have harmed us, not the other way around, but this can change. Mess with us and you will die. This is my sworn oath."

He was getting angry, which was dangerous for Juliette. I pulled it back. "I believe what you say."

"Then, you'll leave the matter where it is?"

It sounded like he wanted to report my decision to someone. He wasn't the puppet master, I was certain of that much. "You know I can't do that. Not while you're threatening Juliette's life. Let her go and I'm gone too. She's only a small part of something much bigger, right? The big machine you just talked about. I'm guessing some kind of trafficking operation. Maybe big, going right to the top. Now you listen to me. None of that is any of my concern. I'm on the road and I want to keep going. But now I have a problem. I made a promise to someone I would bring her sister home safe, or punish everyone who had a part in her kidnapping. Are you still with me?"

"I'm still here."

"See, I don't break my promises. Not ever. Think of my word as strengthened steel. It doesn't get broken, not for anyone. The bad news for you is that I gave Michelle Dupont my word that I would help her find her sister. So, either you give me her sister and I get back on the road, or I track you down, kill you and all your friends, save her sister and then I get back on the road. Your choice. Make it wisely."

He cut the call.

That was always a risk in ramping things up a little, dialling up the heat. Then again, he was a shark, patrolling the waters of my courage. Poking and watching and measuring. He wanted to know how far he could push me. To see if I backed down. Truth was, I couldn't see a certain way to save the girl's life, whether I rolled over or pushed back. At least this way, he had something to think about. The Moroccan shark had to consider if I was a true risk or not. Expend resources checking me out further. If he did, he wouldn't like what he found. I knew that which is why I poked him a little.

Michelle stepped back inside the restaurant, mascara staining her cheeks. She had been crying and had made no attempt to hide it. Outside, Laurent was walking over to a Mercedes taxi cab. He got inside and pulled away fast in the rain. Michelle pulled her chair out and slumped down on it, red face and tired eyes and fists clenched hard. She said nothing.

"What did he say?" I asked.

"You want the good news or the bad news?"

"I'll take whatever you want to get off your chest first."

"Then he is a bastard! He told me he does not want to get involved. He says we don't know what we're fooling with and that we should forget about Juliette. He really said that."

I stared at her in disbelief. She had talked about Gabriel Laurent briefly after she called him on our way over here, but in quiet but respectful tones, certain he would be able to help her. Now, it looked like his refusal to help her find her sister had broken her into pieces. I moved her along to something hopefully less painful.

"And the good news?"

"I never have to see him again."

I smiled. My phone rang again. I reached into my jacket and grabbed hold of it, checking the screen as I brought it up to my head. Unknown caller. Presuming it was another call from Juliette's kidnappers, I decided to shield Michelle and take the call outside. "Give me a second," I said. "It's personal."

I went outside. Shielding the phone from the a light drizzle, I stepped around the corner into the lee of the café and answered the call. I was expecting it to be my Moroccan friend. That just goes to show how wrong you can be sometimes.

"Blake," I said.

"Good evening, Colonel."

"Sparrowhawk. What a pleasant surprise. I thought you'd forgotten all about me."

EIGHTEEN

The cold voice from his previous call had mellowed into softer, rounder tones, but not quite friendly.

"Not at all," he said.

"If you're thinking about asking me out to dinner, you should know in advance the answer will be no."

"I'm glad to see your sense of humour is intact."

"I have a very stubborn personality. The more I'm messed around, the tougher I get. If someone takes something from me, I get it back with interest. It's a burden. Humour helps with that."

"But under the laughs is a very dangerous man driven by the darkest thoughts?"

"You said that, not me. Why have called me?"

"Because I have some information you might like, regarding the telephone call you just had with a mystery man."

I didn't rise to the bait. Whoever Sparrowhawk was, he had some powerful connections, most likely in the leafy, western suburbs of Cheltenham. The call he was referencing was only a few moments old. It also meant he was tracking everything on my phone, including incoming calls, in real-time. This was not hard to do. These days, anyone with an internet connection and a few dollars to spare could use a third-party app to monitor anyone else's mobile phone. All they needed was the number. Not even jailbreaking the phone was necessary anymore. If Sparrowhawk was working at GCHQ as I suspected, all of this would be child's play. I even considered it possible that he had a live satellite on my present location. I decided to roll with it. Go along to get along.

"You have a name?" I asked.

"I have better than that, but yes. I have a name."

After a pause, I said, "Is this like twenty questions, or do you just tell me?"

"The man you were talking to is Mahjoubi Amzazi, a middle-ranking Moroccan drug trafficker who cut his teeth bringing low-grade hashish into Spain via the Strait of Gibraltar back in the nineties. Born in Marrakech but educated in international schools in Switzerland thanks to his father's tungsten mine in the Rif region. Arrested in 2002 for drugs trafficking and sentenced to sixteen years, reduced to eight years thanks to some paternal influence and cash. Served his time at the maximum-security facility in Kenitra. Within five years on the outside, he was sentenced to another three years for yet more drug smuggling charges and also some bribery charges. Since 2018, he's been based in Málaga, enjoying his new-found freedom, graduating from drugs into human trafficking."

"But is he available for children's parties?"

"There's that humour again."

I stepped around the corner and peered inside the café, making sure Michelle was okay. She hadn't moved but was now drinking from the beer bottle. "You said you have better than a name. What is it?"

"Straight to the point. I like it."

"From my point of view, we're still not at the point."

A shallow laugh. "I told you Amzazi was based in Málaga, but he's not there tonight."

Now it dawned on me. "Where did he make that call from?"

"From a townhouse in Barbès-Rochechouart, in Paris."

A break, at last. Fekir had given me an address in this part of the city, and I was sure I'd just heard Juliette's voice on the phone. This meant she was still in the city and we still had a fighting chance to track her down and rescue her from a specific address before Amzazi got her out of the country. But if they got away before I could get to her, I needed to know more.

"What route does he use to get kidnapped victims out of France?" I asked.

"It's impossible to know them all, but his favourite

appears to be waiting a few days after the kidnapping, and then driving them south to Spain, usually on backroads. We know he's been sighted in Bourges and Limoges. No surprises there, they're both en route to the Spanish border. He has also been seen at the ferry terminal in Algeciras, after that, in Africa, he's somewhat more elusive. He drives from Ceuta to Tangier, but then he's gone – hidden by an impressive network of traffickers and smugglers with contacts all over Morocco. Rabat, Casablanca, Marrakesh, you name it, he could go anywhere. To say he's like the proverbial needle in a haystack would be a gross understatement."

"In other words, if we let him get that far, he's gone for good, and so is the girl."

"You said that, not me."

"I'm guessing you have access to substantial intelligence resources, Sparrowhawk. If Amzazi gets the girl to Morocco, is she gone for good?"

"Yes."

"What happens to her there?"

"She could be sold to anyone, though most likely someone in Africa or the Middle East. If you want to save her life, Blake, it's now or never, old chap. Are you able to handle it all on your lonesome?"

"If you know me as well as you claim to, Sparrowhawk, then you'll know that I shall either find a way or make one."

"Hannibal. As a former classics scholar, I do enjoy a good classical reference. But what I meant was, how are you set up for hardware?"

"I've got it covered," I said, thinking of Bonzo Butler. After retiring from the service, the former SBS sergeant had moved into the delicate world of supplying arms to British operatives in France. I'd worked with him on several missions, back in the SAS and in D19. He was a solid character I knew I could trust, but I wondered why Sparrowhawk was sniffing around trying to find a lamppost to piss on. "But thanks for your concern. Any word on JQ?"

"Mr Quartermain's signal went dead a little while ago, but I'm working on getting that fixed."

"Satellites, ground ops?"

"Ask no questions and you'll be told no lies."

"In that case, I'll say thanks and goodbye."

"In that case, I'll wish you luck and hang up."

The line cut and I checked my watch. It told me time was running out.

NINETEEN

We crossed over the street and walked away from the steamy Café de la Paix. Bonzo's place was one of the Haussmann buildings directly opposite the café. These places were usually divided into several separate apartments, often letting for large sums due to their being so highly sought-after, but Bonzo's trading in arms over the years had enabled him to purchase an entire building just for himself. Its steeply sloped, grey mansard roof was slick with rainwater and a row of traditional dormer windows reflected the city lights. I knew Bonzo would be back in his house by now. It was past the time he'd asked me to turn up. He'd be set up on the top floor inside one of those fifth-floor windows and keeping a very close eye on me, or more specifically my companion. He knew me. He trusted me. But I knew Bonzo would never rule out the possibility of my having been compromised.

We walked up the short path and I knocked on the door. The front door opened almost immediately to reveal a man in his fifties, short and squat. He'd been fit once but he was running a little to fat around the middle. He wore a black Harley Davidson t-shirt and a pair of blue jeans with badly frayed hems. Tattooed arms. Bare feet. A big, honest smile as he stuck out his hand and nearly pulled me into the hallway. This was Sergeant Frederick "Bonzo" Butler, RM, SBS, Retd.

"Bill, you ugly old bastard. It's good to see you, mate."

"Likewise, Bonzo. This is Michelle."

"Hello, Michelle. What's a nice girl like you doing with a toerag like Bill Blake?"

"This is how he talks about senior officers," I said with a grin.

"And that's in front of their faces," Bonzo boomed. "You can imagine what I say about the arseholes behind their backs."

Michelle cracked a faint smile. It was the first I'd seen since meeting her at the Gare du Nord. Then, a big Alsatian came barrelling down the stairs towards us.

"This is Gustav," Bonzo said. "Gustav, this is Lieutenant Colonel William Blake and Michelle."

Michelle patted his head and stroked his neck as Bonzo closed the door and turned some locks and slid various bolts. "Can't be too careful in my line of work, Bill. Sure you understand. Now then, you two in a hurry?"

"You might say our mission is time-critical," I said.

"In that case, let's move this along. Martina is in the

kitchen making some pasta. You got time to eat?"

"We had some cheese balls in the Café de la Paix," Michelle said.

"So, we'd love to," I said. "But we haven't got much time. I'll tell you about it when we eat."

Bonzo's smile widened. "Cheese balls and now rigatoni alla carbonara. You always were a greedy bastard, Bill. C'mon – both of you. Get out of those wet coats and get some decent homecooked grub down you."

He ushered us to the back of the house and into a well-appointed step-down kitchen. It was large and white with two tall sash windows on the opposite wall to the door. The windows were covered in steam from the cooking pasta and sauce. Martina smiled and waved from across the room and then drained the pasta. She was slim and blonde and at least twenty years younger and five inches taller than Bonzo.

"Met her in Strasbourg," Bonzo said by way of explanation. He started laying a couple more places at the table. Took some wine glasses out of a glass-front cabinet. "But she's from Bratislava. She can't speak great English, but I regale her with my exploits in pidgin French. She's a good lass."

Martina turned around holding two plates of steaming pasta. "I speak better English than he knows."

Bonzo laughed as he brought the other two plates across to the table. "Now she tells me."

We sat down and started eating. Bonzo told Gustav to get in his basket in the corner and as the big dog settled, the former Commando poured four glasses of red wine. He took a sip, smacked his lips and sighed happily. Then, his smile faded and he fixed his eyes on me. "So, tell Uncle Bonzo all about it."

"It's my sister," Michelle said. "She is an independent journalist working on something big, and yesterday she was kidnapped by some very dangerous people. I want to get her home safely. Bill is helping me."

Martina frowned. "That's a terrible story. What are the police doing?"

"The police can't help us," I said.

"I don't understand," said Martina.

Bonzo grew more serious. "If the police aren't part of the solution, they must be part of the problem. Am I right or am I right?"

"You're right," Michelle said. "The people who took my sister are involved in a very high-level people trafficking operation. We're talking government-level officials, including senior police."

Martina put down her fork and shook her head. "I can't believe what I'm hearing. Is this really true?"

Michelle poked her food around for a second or two and then gave up, setting the fork down beside her plate and sighing. "It's true."

"Hell's bells, Blakey," Bonza said. "You're up to your neck in it now, son."

"Which is why I'm here."

He held up his hands and shook his head. "No way, I can supply some tasty weapons and since it's you I'll waive the fee if you bring them back nice and shiny, but I'm not in the muscle game anymore. I've got Martina. And Gustav. He's like a son to me. He'd be gutted if anything happened to me."

"I just need the hardware, Bonzo. I can handle the rest on my own."

Bonzo considered this, then nodded. "And I bet you can, old son. What do you need?"

"I'm relying on an old Beretta right now. The previous owner wasn't the sort of guy to take care of his weapon and it's got a bit of a problem with light strikes."

"Firing pin?"

I shook my head. "No."

He thought about it. "Probably a buggered recoil spring. I can do better than that. As it happens, my supplier in Geneva has just delivered some shiny new toys. Glock 19, do ya? Or maybe a SIG P229?"

"Glock's got a bigger mag."

"By two rounds, let's not wet our pants."

"Those two rounds are the ones that save your life."

He weighed that up. "But the SIG looks cooler. You can't

top that. Plus, it's got better night sights and soaks up recoil better."

"Have you bought shares in them or something, Bonzo?"

He laughed and drank some more wine. Martina and Michelle were looking on, amused.

"Selling guns is my meat and potatoes, Blakey. I'm just telling you how it is."

"And firing them at people is my meat and potatoes," I said with a smile. "I like a consistent trigger pull so I'll go with the striker-fired Glock rather than the hammer-fired SIG. Thanks all the same."

He shrugged. "There goes my dividend."

I laughed and ate some pasta. "Besides, the Regiment is using the Glock 17 now, as do D19."

"Pfft," he said. "I heard the Regiment smoked you out, son."

I paused, unsure of how much to tell him, especially in the company of two people I had known for such a short time. "It's true that we parted company."

"What happened?"

"Things got political."

"A little bird on a wire told me you popped Mulgrave."

"Not here, Bonzo," I said quietly.

A tense pause, and then he poured more wine. "Right then, if you two ladies would like some homemade tiramisu, it's right in the fridge. Martina makes a mean tiramisu. It must be her Slovakian heritage."

Martina laughed, lightening the mood. "If you want a traditional Slovakian dessert, then I'll make you some makovník someday. In the meantime, you have Italian tiramisu because you asked me to make you Italian food tonight!"

Bonzo chuckled, finished his wine with a big slurp and got up from the table. "Never get on the wrong side of a Slovak, Blakey." He kissed Martina on the cheek and transported two of the plates over to the draining board and then gestured for me to follow him out of the room.

"I'll just be a minute," I told Michelle. "Enjoy the tiramisu."

TWENTY

In the hall, Bonzo turned, while walking backwards. "Five floors," he said. "And they're all mine. The house that Glock built. And SIG, Heckler & Koch, B&T, Colt, CZUB, Zastava, Ruag, Diehl, Nammo… you name it, and I've got it. If I haven't got I, I can get it." He laughed and turned around at the bottom of the stairs, grabbing the newel post and bounding up the stairs. "Come on up, old son. The toys are in the attic." Turning on the first landing and relaunching himself up the next flight, he laughed again. "One of my fave albums that one, so the joke never gets old."

At the top of the house, he grabbed a pole hook resting up against a bookcase and used it to pop open the loft hatch. Then he pushed the hook into a hoop at the bottom of the loft ladder and pulled it down to the carpet. Clicking it into place, he slowly climbed up into the loft and switched on the lights. I followed him up and was dumbstruck by the sight. The Haussmann buildings were big buildings with large loft spaces. This was more like a top storey than a loft space. The ceiling was high enough for us to stand and the small dormer windows I'd seen running along the front were repeated on the other side. A central aisle ran down the centre of the loft, dividing the space into two, each side stacked high with boxes stamped with the insignia of various arms manufacturers.

"I'm impressed," I said.

He pointed over to the left. "Your Glock's over there. And now we're out of the way you can give me the full story. You must think this woman is still alive or you wouldn't be wasting your time. Am I right or am I right?"

"She's alive, or at least she was less than an hour ago. I spoke to the men who snatched her and they brought her to the phone for a second. I haven't told Michelle that yet. I might not."

"In case you get her hopes up?"

I nodded. "Still, I think it was her."

"How did you know it was her?"

"Before I spoke, she thought I was Michelle and called me Mimi. Michelle told me earlier that she always calls her Mimi. If she was acting, she was a bloody good actor, mate. I suppose it could be a setup, but not sure the men behind this would bother."

"Juice not worth the squeeze, sort of thing?"

I nodded. "Right."

He handed me the Glock and opened up some fresh boxes of ammunition. "Why are you doing this, Bill?"

"Because I can."

He paused and sat down on the side of a boxful of armour-piercing, hollow-charge forty-mil Diehl ammo as if it were an armchair. Then he pulled a green glass ashtray out of the shadows, balanced it on a box of hand grenades just beside him and lit up a Camel. He offered me one and I took it. He opened one of the dormer windows behind him and we smoked together in silence for a while, then he said, "I know what happened with Mulgrave, Bill. I know you took him out and I know you got flushed from D19. The Regiment has washed its hands of you and cut you loose and now you're out in the cold."

"You're very well informed."

"I'm Bonzo Butler. Purveyor of the finest arms and incendiary devices in Europe. You get to meet some very interesting people in my line of work. Men and women very much plugged into the Matrix, Bill. I know everything. I have to, it's my meat and potatoes. It's how I bring home the bacon for our pasta dishes. You think Martina would hang around with a bloke like me if I didn't have all this?"

"Of course she wouldn't," I said. "You're way too ugly."

"That's more like it. Now we're on the same page. Singing from the same hymn sheet. Shitting in the same latrine. When all this is over, are you going to stay in Paris?"

"Why? You have a job for me?"

"Just asking."

I shook my head and took a drag on the Camel. "When you said I was out in the cold, well it's worse than that."

He raised his chin and flicked some ash into the ashtray. "How much worse?"

"It's not just out in the cold. I'm on the run."

"The bastards burned you?"

"Mulgrave put a termination order on me before I killed him." I inhaled more smoke and blew it out through the small dormer window. "Quartermain."

His eyes flicked up to me and his face hardened. "They put Jack Quartermain on your tail?"

"Yes."

"That's not very polite."

"I take it you know him, you being an old SBS lag and all."

He nodded. "I know him. He was an old school bootneck. Nasty piece of work. The sort of man you learn fast not to go out drinking with. Fights and brawls follow him around like lost puppies. He tried to get in the SBS a couple of times but always failed. Gave up eventually."

"Why did he fail?"

"Not physical stamina, believe me. He was the toughest we ever had. That man would tolerate any conditions for any length of time. And he had real guile, too. Just what we're always looking for. It's even in our nifty little motto, so it must be true. He was a real ruthless and sneaky bastard, but the problem with Jack was his temperament." Bonzo tapped his temple. "He was always a few ham rolls short of a picnic. Unpredictable, unstable, and getting worse with age. Can't have that sort of thing in outfits like ours. You ever meet him?"

"I worked with him a long time ago. I know what he's capable of."

"I didn't know the stupid bastard was doing hits for Her Maj though." He gave a sad laugh and shook his head, sucked on his cigarette. "Ordered to kill by a man now dead and yet still on his mission. Silly sod thinks he's the Terminator. You can take him out, Bill. But watch your back."

I nodded. "Yeah."

"You know where he is?"

"In Paris."

"How do you know that?"

"A little bird on a wire told me."

He smiled. "What happens when you save the girl? You fly off into the sunset with Michelle? She's pretty. Way out of your league, old son."

"After this is all over, I want to say goodbye to someone."

"Your wife?"

I nodded. "I haven't even been to her grave, Bonzo. We can talk sunsets after that."

He sensed the atmosphere and leapt up, stubbing out his

cigarette and clapping his hands. “You’ve got the Glock, you’ve got some ammo. Anything else?”

“Got any GPS trackers? Magnetic is best.”

He rummaged around in a box and threw a fresh box at me. “All yours. Anything else?”

“I’ll take a good quality combat knife.”

“You don’t fancy a submachine gun? I’ve got fifty per cent off some MP7s.”

“No, that’ll do for now. I don’t think these guys are too heavily armed. Not from what I’ve seen so far, anyway. That'll do.”

“You want to keep things intimate, personal. I understand. Now, Any more questions?”

I stubbed out my cigarette and stood up. “Yeah. What the hell is makovník, Bonzo?”

“No idea, mate,” he said with a shrug. “No bloody idea at all.”

TWENTY-ONE

A storm was gathering in the skies above Paris. Michelle drove us out to the address Fekir had given me and Sparrowhawk had confirmed. Around a hundred yards shy of the place, I told her to pull up and stay in the car. I had the Glock now, so I gave her the Beretta and showed her how to use it and what its quirks were. Then I told her to lock the doors and get the hell away if anything went wrong. She was not a naïve woman and she had spent a short time in the Paris police, but I wasn't confident that she stood much of a chance with men like we were dealing with tonight. I got out and closed the door, the cold, rainy air whipping over me and stinging my eyes. I pulled up my collar and walked the rest of the way, keeping in the shadows of a high concrete wall running alongside the road.

Barbès-Rochechouart was not a good part of Paris. It was a dangerous, dirty quarter of the city. Rows of poorly maintained terraces with barred windows, shop-shutters sprayed with graffiti, dog excrement on the pavements. Upturned rubbish bins in the street, litter blowing in the wind. Broken houses were packed in tight on the hills and divided by steep, winding stone steps, also fouled by dogs and plastered in graffiti. Not on the typical tourist trail, but I thought it was probably a good match for Amzazi. The Moroccan could of course afford much better and would have lived somewhere considerably smarter. This was his workplace. This was where he brought his victims while his superiors decided their fates.

I passed a short row of closed shops and turned left, following a short series of stone steps down to the address I needed. Approaching the target location, I walked past a man and a woman in a darkened doorway. He was smoking a cigarette. She turned and stared at me, their faces white in a stripe of streetlight. I drifted past them, hands in pockets, turning my head away and leaving them to whatever they were doing. I wanted them in my life even less than they wanted me in theirs.

According to the address details I had been given, Amzazi's place was a minute or two further down the road. I turned and checked behind me. No one following. No cameras in sight. Looked like I was going to be unannounced, my preferred method of introduction. I found an arched entrance at the side of the property that looked like it led around to the back garden, probably for use wheeling rubbish bins out to the street on collection day. I turned into it, pulling the Glock from my old barn coat, gambling it was going to take me around to the back.

Dark now, off the street and away from the lights. As my vision adjusted to the darkness, I reached the end of the passageway and saw it opened onto a patio area filled with assembled junk kept out of the weather by a large plastic tarp. Beyond it, unmown ankle-high grass on a lawn full of weeds and littered with old, damp cardboard boxes was the full extent of a small garden. High fences, some broken. Neighbouring properties stretched up on all sides, making it feel like more of a tenement courtyard than a garden. A dog barked behind me. I swung the gun around and aimed low. It barked again, from the property next door, behind a fence. I saw its muzzle snapping and snarling in an inch of clearance at the bottom of the fence, rotted away by wet weather. It couldn't get to me, no matter how angry it was. Lucky dog.

I moved out into the garden a few steps and looked up at Amzazi's house. The windows were barred, as I had expected, but the rear door was not. I guessed this door was locked, but above it on the next floor was a wide hung balcony and a set of French doors. Beneath the balcony on top of one of the tarps were dozens of cigarette butts. Seemed to me like these guys liked to smoke out on the balcony and the door behind it was probably open. This seemed more promising. Two lights were on – one downstairs in the room to the left of the door, and one upstairs. I heard quiet music, disposable radio trash, coming from the upstairs room and the sound of people talking in Arabic.

It was time.

I slowly pushed on the downstairs door just in case. It was locked, which had been expected. Plan B involved me climbing up onto the shed roof and jumping across to the hung balcony. I grabbed the rails, slick with rain and vaulted over onto the balcony, barn coat flapping out behind me in the night. On my feet now, I tried the upper floor door. It was open, also to be expected given the cigarette butts. This room was dark, and I stepped inside. I smelled cannabis immediately, drifting in through the open door on the far side of the room. The rest of the room was unimpressive. More cardboard boxes mostly sealed up with packaging tape. Some old coats and a stack of greasy pizza boxes. An old cathode-ray TV set from another age in the corner beside a DVD player and a pile of discs, some in cases, others spilt out on the floor. Recently emptied ash trays on both arms of a worn-out vinyl sofa facing the TV. On the wall above the sofa, a Pirelli calendar, displaying October 2018.

The storm broke with a wild flash of lightning that strobed the room with blinding light for a few seconds. A roar of thunder shook the house. I walked over to the internal door, gun raised into the aim and ready for kick-off. The smell of fatty lamb and cumin and garlic floated up the stairs in front of me. The Arabic voices in the lit room next door were clearer now. They were speaking in the Moroccan dialect. I struggled to catch nearly any of it; the accent and dialect were too distant from what I had learnt. I caught the word *Marlboro*, and then the words for *cigarettes* and *buy* buried in an otherwise alien sentence. The door opened. A short man in a cheap leather jacket stepped out into the corridor at the top of the stairs.

I stepped back into the dark room. He hadn't seen me and now walked down the corridor and turned to go down the stairs. Probably Moroccan, thirties, a little overweight. Scraggly beard and lots of gold jewellery, he was soon out of sight. After a gust of cold air came up the stairs, I heard the front door slam shut. He had gone out to buy his cigarettes. He'd spent his life being told smoking would kill him one day. Tonight, they had saved his life.

Into the room he'd just vacated. Two more men, sitting on another cheap couch. One thin and one fat, they were watching adult entertainment on a plasma TV. I whistled and they turned, scrambling for weapons. The big one reached for a knife and the little one stuffed his hand inside his jacket, most likely in the search for a gun.

"No, no, no," I said, sweeping the gun's barrel from one startled face to another. "Hands where I can see them. Now."

TWENTY-TWO

They obeyed.

"I'm looking for Mahjoubi Amzazi."

The thin one's eyes darted to the fat one, which told me what I wanted to know. I turned the gun on the thin one and let him have the Mozambique Drill. Two in the chest and one in the head. The shots rang out almost impossibly loud in the small residential room. His bloody body slumped to the floor in front of the TV and started to bleed out on the floorboards. Smoke drifted from the muzzle. Amzazi stared down in horror at the bullet-pocked forehead of his associate, recoiling in fear and nearly falling out of his chair.

"Hands back up, Mahjoubi, or you go out the same way."

"Who the hell are you?" he managed.

"You don't remember me? I'm offended. We talked a few minutes ago."

Confusion and fear washed out his face. "I don't understand…"

"How I got here so fast? You might say I have friends in low places. Now, where is the girl?" I asked, teeth gritted.

"What girl?"

I shot him in the kneecap, blasting it to pieces. He shrieked like a child and reached down to the wound, rolling off the chair and crashing into the floorboards, inches from the dead man.

"Where is Juliette Dupont? Now."

A rank, coarse laugh surprised me. "She is gone, stranger. Gone in the night. You will never find her."

"You'd be amazed how resourceful I can be. Where is she, or you'll limp on both sides for the rest of your life, instead of just the one."

The chuckle quietened down and his face grew soberer. "I already told you. She's gone."

"Last time, Amzazi. Where has she gone?"

He looked at the gun's muzzle, aiming at his other kneecap and swallowed hard. "And if I tell you, you will let me live?"

"We'll have to assess the quality of your information first."

He thought about it and sighed. Looking at his wrecked knee, gone forever, he gave way. "All right, you win. I will tell you where she went – but this does not mean you will find her. After your threats to get her back, the decision was made to move her on fast. She is very valuable to my employer. Much more valuable than most of the meat that we smuggle."

My stomach turned at the word, but I stayed focused. "Who do you work for, Amzazi?"

I thought he was going to talk, but then he thrust his arm under the chair. He was reaching for something. I presumed it was a weapon. A knife, maybe a firearm. Reluctantly, I fired three shots into his head and killed him. I walked over to the chair and crouched down. He had been reaching for a mobile telephone. I probably should have let him live. Now, I had ended the trail. I picked up the phone and looked at it but it was password protected. Something told me Amzazi wasn't going to let me know what it was, but I slipped it in my pocket all the same. It might yield something, after all. I considered Sparrowhawk and his contacts. Maybe one of them might be able to do something with it.

I left Amzazi's obese corpse cooling back on the vinyl sofa, the adult film still flickering in the dark behind him. Somewhere below me, some music cranked up. It was a deep, rhythmic bass that sounded like it was maybe coming from the ground floor. Time to go. Down the stairs, gun in the aim. Keen to avoid the Marlboro Man, I headed for the back door. I could use the alley at the side of the house and get back to Michelle in less than five minutes. Through the kitchen and past the cooking lamb. The music was louder now but coming from below me. Then, as I was considering the possibility of a basement, I heard someone screaming out. It was a woman's voice, sad and desperate. Hoarse. I froze in the darkness, gun gripped in my hand. She was speaking in a mix of Arabic and French but I couldn't identify her location. It sounded like it was coming from beneath me.

A basement then. I hadn't seen any women in this house, after all, and yet if it was supposed to be one of the operation's, they had to be somewhere. Before I could pinpoint the screaming, a fourth man entered the house. He was not the man who had gone to buy cigarettes, but someone else, younger and fitter. Not north African, but European. He was more surprised to see me than the other way around and I had the advantage.

He drew a blade from somewhere inside a denim jacket. I didn't want to kill him in case he had information so for now, taking his life was an unnecessary risk. I holstered the gun and grabbed hold of the cooking saucepan on the stove. I flung the hot food in his face. He ducked and most went up the wall behind him. Some went in his face. He grunted in shock and pain and wiped it from his stinging eyes, giving me time to turn the pan on its side and bring it around hard in a wide arc, slamming it into the side of his head.

He crashed back against the countertop, losing his knife as he went. I kicked the blade out of the kitchen into the dark room behind him. He reached for a knife block and pulled out a long boning knife, waving it in my face, pain and hate etched deep on his face. I was still holding the saucepan and now took a step towards him.

He rotated his upper body, the boning knife still in his hand. He pulled his arm back and brought the knife slashing through the air towards my face.

I brought the heavy pan up and blocked the attack just in time, forcing the long blade to crash into the copper base of the pan with a loud metallic scratching noise. I continued moving the pan forward, turning the blocking action into an offensive move and forcing his knife hand back against the countertop. At the same time, I powered a hefty headbutt into his face and broke his nose. This time he screamed out in pain and dropped the knife again, bringing both hands up to his face instinctively to check the damage.

I gave no quarter, bringing the pan back up and cracking him on his left temple, knocking him out cold and driving his unconscious body down onto the floor where it sank in a heap. I tossed the pan down on his stomach and began my search for the basement.

TWENTY-THREE

The music's bass beat boomed louder, a constant thudding as I searched for the source of the woman's screams. I realised they were coming from the house next door. I crossed a junk-strewn sitting room at the back of the house and found an adjoining door. It was unlocked and I opened it and looked into the other house. When I saw the Marlboro Man standing talking to another man, both of whom were ignoring the screams, it was immediately obvious Amzazi owned this one too and that he was using it as some kind of club.

Both men turned and looked at me. Then, they reached for concealed weapons under their jackets. They never stood a chance. I fired on them, controlled bursts, three shots into each and dropped them both where they stood at the bottom of some stairs. Then, I made my way past their bodies, following the sound of the screams as they led me to the back of the house. I tracked along a narrow corridor until I reached a back room. I saw a wall covered in old, torn posters. The stench of pine disinfectant from an open toilet, the smell of stale beer. I tried a closed door. It was locked but flimsy, so I put it in with my boot and stepped inside. Nothing.

Back outside, gun in hand but still no one around. Up ahead was a black door. I opened it and rushed inside and drew my gun up into the aim. Black-painted walls covered in posters for old punk bands, naked light bulbs. A naked light bulb hanging from a wire in the centre of the ceiling. A door, open and leading to a flight of stairs descending into darkness. A small man was walking up the steps, he was holding a tray of empty cups and bowls in his hands. I stepped forward so the light bulb was directly behind me, just above my head. On the top step, he stopped and looked up at me, squinting.

"Pierre, is that you?"

In the Old West, they called it buffaloing. These days it goes by the term pistol-whipping. It just means using a handgun to manually deliver a heavy blow, usually to the face. Turning it from sidearm to blunt instrument. My old drill sergeant back in the Paras told me it all started in the days of the old muzzle loaders. Those old firearms only took one round at a time, loaded up through the barrel and when it was spent the next best thing to do was use the damn thing like a knuckle duster. It was a substantial act, often rendering the victim unconscious.

That's what happened to Pierre's friend, anyway. The

grip of the Glock landed right on target on his right temple, delivered at the end of a long, fast swinging arc that came at him out of the dazzling light behind me. The impact cracked something in his temple and knocked him clean out. He dropped the tray and fell back down the steps into the dark, tumbling all the way to the bottom as the bowls and cups clattered and rolled all over the floor at my boots.

I kicked them back inside the door, stepped inside and found another light. The thumping bass of the music had veiled the noise of the tray going down and the sound of the man falling down the stairs, but sooner or later, he would be missed. No sense leaving a trail. I closed the door and made my way down the stairs. At the bottom, I stepped over the unconscious man and swept the gun in an arc. All clear. I was standing in some kind of storage space. Another door ahead. If the basement ran the entire length of both houses, it would be a large and labyrinthine space to search.

I went through and found what looked like some kind of office. It was occupied by a man in a suit jacket and t-shirt. Startled, he took one look at me and the gun and opened his top drawer. No prizes for guessing what he kept in there. I told him to raise his hands. He ignored me. I swung the Glock up into the aim and buried two rounds in his forehead. I was leaping over his body a second after he hit the floor and swinging the gun around into the next room. It was clear. Back out into the corridor and padding down to the next room. A man leaned out with a gun in his hand. He was just far enough inside the door to stop a headshot, then he fired at me. As his bullet traced past me, I dropped into a crouching position and fired on his gun hand, obliterating his first two knuckle sockets and forcing him to drop the weapon. He pulled his hand into this body and slipped back into the room. I gave chase, firing two rounds into his back. He dropped like a stone. It was all over very fast.

I went through into the main part of the basement, slow and easy. Gun in the aim. The place was green thanks to an emergency exit light but that was the only illumination. The place smelt of oil and sulphur and perfume. The woman's screaming had stopped. I guessed she had drawn too much attention to herself and someone had shut her up. I made my way over to the door kicked it open with my riot boot and it smashed back against its hinges sending a shower of splinters and dust bursting into the newly opened doorway. I stormed into the room and swept the gun from side to side, finding a man in a chair fumbling for a weapon somewhere at his side. Just like with the other guy, I fired two rounds into his forehead and ended the search, then crossed the room and reached the door he was supposed to be guarding. I thumbed the mag release on the left side of the grip and ejected it. I reached into my pocket. New mag in hand, I smacked it in the grip and went on.

Whoever was inside would have heard the shots. They'd be ready and waiting.

But not for me.

Second door smashed in and I tucked myself into a diving roll. Bullets chased me across the room and I came to a stop behind a long black couch. The first thing I noticed was some kind of fire exit off to my right. First job, swing my gun over the back of the couch and take out the naked bulb light hanging in the centre of the ceiling. A door to my right burst open. It was close to me and the two men were on top of me in seconds. No guns. I swung up the muzzle to fire but it was too late. The first guy punched it out of my hand. Disarmed meant fisticuffs. I lunged closer, right arm bent at the wrist, elbow thrust back into the man's throat. When the elbow was pushed hard into his windpipe, I swung my forearm upwards and smashed the back of my hand into his face, crushing his nose. He stepped back, not wanting more. I rotated at the waist and brought my left leg up, driving my boot into his right temple. He went down hard.

The other guy grabbed my shoulder and spun me around. This bloke looked Scandinavian, Finnish maybe. He was a giant slab of hardened muscle like a side of grass-fed Hereford beef. He came at me with both arms outstretched, curling his meaty hands into two tight fists of steel. He threw a punch. Right hook, easily dodged. When the punch ran out of energy, I grabbed his wrist and twisted it hard counter-clockwise, grinding the radius and ulna bones together until I felt them snap like two dry twigs. He screamed out, I powered my left fist into his face and made contact with the soft part of his cheek and the maxillary bone. It hurt both of us, but him more. The force of the blow drove his head back to my right, away from me. He was stunned. I grabbed his broken wrist, spun him around and pinned his arm against his back in a V, bringing his hand up almost to his neck. Then I forced him forward and drove his face into the corner of a steel filing cabinet rail, taking him out of the fight with a bone-splintering impact of face-on-metal.

The woman screamed again. It was coming from the next room. I heard a man shouting, a slap and then the screaming stopped. I doubted it was Juliette because of the Arabic I'd heard, but whoever she was, she needed help and fast. I pulled the handle down and entered the room. Two leather sofas, ash trays balanced on the arms. Butts in the trays and fresh smoke in the air but no sigh of anyone. A glass that smelt of vodka on a table next to the sofa on my right. A door was on my left and then I heard men arguing in Arabic and a hoarse, terrified scream from behind it. It was now or never.

TWENTY-FOUR

I stepped over to the door, gun gripped in both hands and worked through my options. It was not a great position, but better than being in the middle of the room if someone was about to open the door. No one did. I decided to break the door down and go into the room. I took a step back and raised my right leg, bent at the knee. Then I smashed the door open with my riot boot and tucked myself down into a diving roll. Splintered wood exploded in a cloud and the door handle flew off, rolling away to the right.

Into the room in the roll and up onto my feet, swinging around in an arc, sweeping the gun in a steady line, one hundred and eighty degrees from wall to wall. Two men, the men I had heard arguing, were sitting at either end of the sofa, a crying woman in between them. I discharged my weapon into each man, starting with the man on my right who was leaner, and consequently, faster. Failure drill, two rounds to the chest and one to the head. He slumped onto the woman, making her scream all over again in horror. The other guy struggled to pull some kind of weapon from inside his jacket. I never found out what it was. I fired two bullets into his chest and one to the head, spraying a sheet of blood out over the wall behind him. He slumped down to his side, away from the woman.

She was Middle Eastern, maybe Syrian or Lebanese. I beckoned to her and raised a hushed finger to my lips. She slipped on her shoes, which were down on the floor in front of the sofa, and made her way across the room. Her face was tight with fear as she approached me. She tried to talk in a whisper, just a few words of broken French but I shushed her again and gestured towards the door. Taking her hand, I ran back out to where I had seen the fire escape and kicked open the panic bar. Outside, we were at the bottom of a steep set of concrete steps leading back up to ground level. Still holding her hand, I led her up the steps and away from the property, out into the rain-lashed night.

"Who are you?" she asked in heavily accented French.

"A friend and I need your help. But not now and not here."

"You saved my life! My name is Fatima."

"No more words." I ran with her back to the car. Michelle was shocked when she saw us coming. She clambered out of the car, a look of confusion on her face when she took in the mascara-streaked face of the young woman with me.

"Get back in," I called out. Michelle did as I said and got back into the car. I opened the back door and Fatima piled in. I slammed the door and ran around to the front passenger seat. "Go."

Michelle hit the accelerator, spinning the wheels on the slick tarmac. The car juddered and squealed as she cornered the road at speed and then we were gone, effortlessly lost in the meandering backroads of deepest Paris. "What the hell happened in there?"

"Keep driving," I said. "We'll talk when we pull over."

That was twenty minutes later in the next arrondissement. She pulled up into a side street just north of the Louvre and rolled to a quiet stop, close enough to see the glow of the famous museum in the sky through the windscreen. She switched off the engine and the wipers stopped moving halfway across the glass.

"What happened, Bill?" she asked. "And who is this woman?"

"This is Fatima," I said. "I found her in Amzazi's basement back in his townhouse."

Michelle turned in her seat and looked at the woman. "My God, I'm so sorry. Are you all right?"

Fatima nodded. "I will be now. I don't know how to thank you."

"How long had you been down there?" Michelle asked.

"Not long. A few days. I am from Tunisia, but they said they were taking me to Berlin. They put me on some kind of internet slave market."

Michelle looked like she was going to be sick.

Fatima said, "Please, why did you save me?"

"We're looking for someone," I said.

"My sister," Michelle said. "We're looking for my sister. We think she was taken by the same people that took you. If I show you a picture, maybe…" She fumbled in her purse and handed Fatima the folded image of her sister.

The Tunisian looked at the picture and shook her head. "I don't think so."

"Her name is Juliette. She would be a little older now. Her hair would be different. She dyed it blonde a few weeks ago."

Fatima studied the image a few seconds longer. Then her eyes widened slightly and a light went on behind her eyes. "Yes, I think now that you say this about the hair, maybe I have seen her."

I felt Michelle's desperate eyes crawling all over me. Sensed the hope burning inside her.

"Are you sure?" I asked. "Think carefully. There's a lot at stake."

"I am sure, yes."

"Did she tell you her name?" Michelle asked.

Fatima shook her head. "I never talked to her. She was gagged the whole time she was with me, and her arms tied behind her back. But I think it was her."

Michelle covered her mouth with her hand and turned to

face away. I heard her stifle a sob.

"I think it was her too," I said, thinking back to the phone call I'd had with Amzazi. "How long was she with you?"

"Not long. Hours. Maybe four or five. She was on the same internet slave market as me. I think someone in Morocco bought her."

Michelle smacked her hand down in the steering wheel and cursed. "I will kill them for this."

"Is there anything you can tell us that might help us find her?" I asked.

Fatima thought for a few moments. "No, I don't think so. No – wait, maybe there is."

"What is it?" I said. "Anything could help us, even the smallest detail."

"I heard some men talking when they were setting up the auction. They said they might take the girl – Juliette – down to Morocco by car. They also talked about Provence. I don't know. I could only snatch a few details here and there. Fragments, really."

I turned to her and gave her a reassuring look. "Any other fragments that might help us?"

Fatima said, "They talked about their boss. I think his name was Gobet. Jean Gobet. I think someone said he was in the military. They seemed afraid of him. Let me think. I remember now, they said he was in the Marine Infantry Parachute Regiment. I remember because my brother was a paratrooper back in Tunisia. I think this Gobet is a very tough man. A man who will never talk. Now he runs some kind of import business."

"Did they say where he runs his business?" I asked.

"I heard them talk about a farmhouse at Meaux, but I don't know here that is."

"I do," Michelle said. "It's east of Paris. Not far."

Fatima went quiet. "That is all I know. I'm sorry."

"You've been a lot of help," I said, exchanging a quick look of hope with Michelle. "Now, where do you want to go?"

"Home," she said. "But we can start by calling my brother. He will take me there. He will get me home safe."

"No problem," I said.

"But what about you?" she asked. "What will you do?"

"We're going to have a little chat with Monsieur Gobet."

TWENTY-FIVE

After a short drive. we found the farmhouse. It wasn't hard. Michelle checked some kind of online business register and tracked down Gobet that way. The business was called Gobet Imports and located in a farmhouse three kilometres outside of Meaux in a rural commune mostly dominated by dairy farms. From Paris, we cruised through the French countryside on the autoroute at a level seventy kilometres per hour. Michelle nothing for most of the way. We smoked, windows cranked down an inch. She tuned into a terrible radio station but seemed to like the music so I sucked it up. She needed any distraction she could get. She broke the silence when we reached the farm.

"Bill, I want you to be careful."

I nodded in acknowledgement but said nothing. I was too busy scanning the property which seemed quiet and dark. "The place looks empty."

It was very late in the evening now, and it looked like no one was home. The farm buildings were old and tired and splashed with mud from the recent rainstorm. I was looking for the name given to me by Fatima as some kind of confirmation. Then, ahead on the left, I saw a rust-speckled roller shutter on a warehouse with the name Gobet painted on it. Big red letters in peeling paint on a blue steel door.

"Looks like we got our man," I said. "Pull over. I'll check inside the warehouse first, and then maybe the main farmhouse."

She brought the car to a stop and after pulling a torch from the glove box, I got out. I heard nothing. The wind rippled through some tall dead grass growing up the side of the warehouse. Michelle wandered over to me. I saw two chunky steel shackle padlocks, at least a kilo each in weight, securing its door and turned back to the car. "We're not getting in this way. I'll check the back. Pull over to the side and keep the doors locked."

Around the back, I found a suitable window and put it in with the Glock's grip. After smashing the glass shards clear, I climbed in and landed with a smack inside the warehouse. Its interior was divided into sections by long stretches of industrial shelving racks with interlocking wire decks. Most were empty, but the ones along the far wall were stacked with large wholesale cans of spices and dried figs and Medjool dates. The whole place smelled like cumin or coriander or a mix of them. This was the heart of Gobet's import business, but it was just a façade, covering up the real business. People trafficking.

"Looks like Fatima got everything right," I said, swinging the torch over the stock. I could see an open internal door leading to a narrow corridor. It receded into darkness. "This is a front for the operation, all right. Maybe the main one."

"But where is Juliette?"

"Not in here. Maybe we'll find some clues inside the main house."

"How do we know he's not in there, sleeping?"

"We don't."

I heard tyres crunching on the gravel outside the warehouse and then main beams sweeping across the inside of the warehouse through the window as a car turned and came to a stop outside. We ducked down to avoid the beams.

"Gobet?" Michelle asked.

"Now we know he's not inside sleeping." I watched a man climb out of the car. Shiny black leather jacket and black jeans. Roll neck, black-rimmed glasses, receding hair and grey beard, cut short. Tall, muscular. No flab. I remembered what Fatima told me about his former military background. Looking at him, it was possible.

"That's got to be our man," I said. "Time for a chat."

"But Fatima said Gobet will never talk. She said he was a soldier. She was right about everything else."

"No matter. There are other ways to get the information out of a man who will not talk."

She looked up at me, frowning in the darkness. "What

do you mean?"

"I mean, you stay here and stay out of the way."

"I seem to be doing a lot of that," she said.

"A lot of what?"

"Staying out of the way and doing nothing. Juliette is my sister."

"And Jean Gobet is a former soldier who traffics women to top up his income. He'll be armed and dangerous. It's no good saving your sister's life if you lose yours in the process. Go back to the car, behind the wheel, keys in the ignition and lock the doors. If anything goes pear-shaped, you get the hell out of here."

"Just like normal."

"Just like normal. I'll get you when things are under control."

Before she could complain, I slipped out of the warehouse and made my way towards the main farmhouse. Cream-coloured stone and surrounded by holm oaks and hornbeams. The house was in a slight hollow with a long retaining wall of roughly hewn stones on its southerly aspect and a small river running along its eastern perimeter. Gobet's silver Merc S Series was parked on the big, wide gravel drive. I nipped around it and found some shadows to run in all the way to the expensive glass and steel veranda extension I had seen Gobet use to enter the property. I drew my gun and peered inside.

Gobet was in a large, open vaulted living area, pouring himself a drink from a crystal decanter. No sign of Juliette or anyone else. He walked the tumbler across to a leather sofa, put the glass down on a side table, removed his jacket and then stepped over to a large, expensive desktop computer. He took a flash drive from his pocket, inserted it into the computer and opened some files. Then he saved something and put the flash drive on the desk beside the computer. He yawned and slumped down to rest on the sofa. He closed his eyes. Reached out for the glass and took a sip. It looked like whisky, maybe brandy. The sliding door he had used to gain entry was unlocked. I could tell by looking at the catch on the inside handle. I slid it open and stepped into the room.

TWENTY-SIX

His eyes flashed open and he flailed around on the chair, trying to get to his feet.

"Stay where you are and put your hands in the air," I said in French, approaching him very fast with the gun raised in the aim and pointed directly at his face. "Get your arse back in the chair, now."

He froze, half-up, half-down, then lowered himself down. "I have nothing here of any value. All my valuables are in a vault in Paris."

"I don't want your money," I said.

He looked confused. "Then why are you here?"

"I want Juliette Dupont, now."

His face paled. "I don't know what you're…"

The first shot went into his knee, splintering the patella and blasting a cloud of blood mist and bone fragments up into his face. He screamed in horror, reached out for his knee and rolled over on the chair, crying like a baby.

"Juliette Dupont," I said. "I want her location or you lose the other knee."

"Who are you?" he wailed. "Why are you in my home?"

"I will not ask again."

He rolled over again, turning his tear-streaked face to me. There was a lot of rage in that face. "I will kill you for this."

"Unlikely." I walked over and pushed the gun's muzzle into his temple. "But I will kill you if you don't tell me where she is. Three, two…"

"Not here," he said, trying to shy away from the muzzle. I tracked it along with him and pushed it into his flesh one more time. "She is not here, I swear."

"I did not ask you where she wasn't, Gobet. I asked you where she is."

"I don't know, I swear. She is in the latest batch of girls, but they never came through here. It's a busy business. Some of these latest women come from Paris, others from Strasbourg. They're going out all over the place. I don't know, I swear. Diouf stopped here en route to the south from Poland. I think he's going to pick the Dupont woman up from Paris and take her to Morocco. I know nothing more than this. That's the truth, I swear to you."

"You do a lot of swearing. Who is Diouf?"

"Léon Diouf. He is part of the operation."

"Obviously."

"He works directly for the boss."

"And who is the boss?"

"The man's name is Vaillancourt, Max Vaillancourt. You

are advised to leave him alone. He heads up the operation's security and he will never talk. He has too much to lose. You will not make him talk. He is too important to the operation. He works for some of the most corrupt men in politics in Europe, Russia and America. They all use him. He has a very good reputation."

"Where is Diouf now?"

"I told you, en route to the south, via Paris."

"How far along?"

"I don't know. Sometimes he takes the women out of the loop for a few hours so he can..."

His voice faded.

"Computer password."

"What?"

"Give me your computer password."

He sighed and made a show of resistance. It's not easy, or convincing, to do this when a man has a gun in your face. "Medusa1322. It's no good. Everything here, everything to do with the operation, is encrypted. There is no way in."

With the gun still trained on him, I walked over to the desk and tried the password out. It worked. "What's the file called with all the goodies on it?"

"Goodies?"

"The trafficking op you scumbags are running."

He stared up at the ceiling and winced in pain as he clutched at his knee. "Operation Sirocco."

I found the file and checked what was in it. Word and Excel documents, some scanned documents, contracts, some pictures, Lots of names and addresses. When I opened some of the Word documents, most were encrypted, just as he had said, but some were accessible. New stuff. I transferred them all to the flash drive on his desk and put it in my pocket. "Incriminating stuff. Thanks. Now give me your phone."

He fumbled for it, passing it to me with bloody hands. I wiped the blood off on his jacket. "PIN?"

"8321."

I tried it out and it worked. "Good job you don't have one of those thumbprint IDs or I'd be taking your thumb with me tonight."

He looked at me, aghast "Who are you, stranger?"

"That's on a need-to-know basis. Where is Vaillancourt?"

"I don't know. He lives in the south somewhere. Very rich. Very big house. A villa. Lots of…" he paused a beat. "…parties. I advise you to stay away from him. Very far away."

"Noted," I said and knocked him unconscious with the Glock's grip.

I went back outside and found Michelle. After signalling to her to come over, she drove the car up around to the gravel drive and we went back inside together. When she saw Gobet, knocked out and sprawled on the sofa, his knee obliterated and blood all over his jeans and carpet, she gasped.

"What happened in here?"

"Turned out he needed some persuasion."

"Oh my God! Oh, no, no, no. You have shot another man, Bill! You already killed someone tonight and now you have wounded another!"

She was talking about Rüdiger. I thought it was a good job she hadn't seen what had happened inside the trafficking hub back at Barbès-Rochechouart. "But you're using the word 'man' in its loosest possible sense."

"No, this is wrong."

"You want to find Juliette or not?"

She closed her mouth and nodded. I could she was conflicted. "I'm sorry."

"Forget about it. He had a flash drive on the desk over there. He was looking at something on it. I managed to transfer some files from his desktop onto it as well. Some were already on there, others were not. Some were encrypted, others were not."

She was already going through the drawer in his computer desk. "Here, I found another flash drive. What was his password?"

I told her.

She typed in the password and the computer came to life once again. She put the USB drive into one of the ports and found that this time the USB drive's copy and paste function had been completely disabled.

"We don't have the time to figure out a workaround," I said. "Not now, anyway."

I guessed Gobet was telling the truth when he told me that most of the stuff involving their operation was heavily encrypted. Evidence even close to proving what he was involved in would not be left just lying around for anyone to get hold of, and the few documents I was able to read on the first flash drive were probably accessible because he hadn't had time to organize any encryption. How did I know the evidence was here? Gobet was prepared to take a bullet to keep me in the dark. That's how. You read more in a few seconds from a man's eyes and actions than an hour listening to his words.

"What now?" Michelle asked.

"I need a coffee and then I have a phone call to make. But first, we need to make Monsieur Gobet more comfortable. Find me some tape or rope or cord, please."

TWENTY-SEVEN

After trussing Gobet with some nylon rope and construction tape we found in one of the smaller outbuildings, I made two cups of black coffee on his stovetop coffee percolator and walked them over to Michelle, who was sitting outside on the covered river terrace smoking a cigarette. I sat opposite her with my chair facing the house, river at my back. Just so I could keep an eye over her shoulder on the unconscious man tied up on the sofa in the study inside.

Michelle was disturbed by the sight of Gobet's knee and the blood. Understandable. This is why I had initially told her to stay in the car. Most people like sausages, but not if they ever see them being made. Same goes for a lot of things. A man like Gobet doesn't give up information cheaply. As soon as Fatima told me he was a former Marine Infantry Parachute Regiment squaddie, I knew I had an uphill battle getting what I wanted out of him. I have never worked with RPIMa men before but they have a well-earned reputation for their endurance and strength, like any well-trained SF regiment. Not only that, but this guy was even worse. He was Special Forces gone bad, no doubt with a life of violent crime and abuse stretching out behind him like a ship's wake. He had more to lose. His reputation, his money, his freedom. His life.

Know thine enemy.

She finished her cigarette and sipped the coffee, carefully blowing the top to cool the steaming surface. She looked like she might be slowly getting over what had happened to Gobet. It was an odd thing, how she could feel sympathy for a man who was part of the operation to kidnap and sell her sister on the international slave markets. I didn't understand it. Some people are too good for their own good. A cool breeze blew across the river and rippled her hair.

She wasn't talking to me, at least not yet. I understood. She had formed an image of me in her mind, shaped only by the short time she had known me, but in that time she had never seen the sausage maker. There was nothing I could do about that. We had the intelligence we needed from Gobet, and now he was detained, bound and gagged in his plush study. When he came to, he would be as angry as a nest of wasps. Not my problem. I had what I wanted and if he played me up, he'd get sent back down again. Michelle would have to see that, too.

I drank some coffee. It was much cooler now. Around half a cigarette after that, I said, "The information he was protecting will help us find your sister."

Michelle looked away. "Don't talk to me, please."

I took some more coffee. It wasn't personal, and I didn't feel the need to justify what I had done or make excuses beyond what I had just said to her.

"Have you done that before?" she asked.

I nodded. "I've been in combat, Michelle."

"But still…" Her words faded and she brought the cup up to her lips, taking another sip. The coffee seemed to be calming her down. "You nearly killed him. He could bleed to death."

"He's involved in the kidnap of your sister."

"I know."

Unexpectedly, she brought her hand up from her lap and placed it on mine, on the table. Then, she squeezed it and I felt her other hand on my thigh under the table. She ran her hand along my thigh and then rose from her chair and leaned over the table to kiss me. She paused, an inch from my face, her perfume much stronger now. I noticed her earring glinting in the light from the study behind her.

"You did what you had to," she whispered in French. "I understand."

We kissed momentarily, but she pulled back after a few seconds and sat back down, sweeping her hair back from her face and looking away, finding temporary refuge in the act of fumbling for a second cigarette.

She switched back to English. "I don't know why I just

did that."

"It's okay," I said. "I'm going to make a call now, all right?"

"A call?"

"Before he took his nap, Gobet gave me the name of the man who is driving your sister south. His name is Léon Diouf. I have Gobet's phone here and Diouf's number. I'm going to call him up and see if we can't rattle his cage a bit. All right?"

She nodded slowly, reluctantly. "Oui."

I stuck the cigarette in my mouth and started dialling.

TWENTY-EIGHT

I thumbed through Gobet's contact list until I found Léon Diouf's number. I called it, making sure the speaker function was not on. Michelle had been through enough tonight without finding out the hard way if anything had happened to Juliette.

When Diouf answered the phone, he was not happy.

"Why are you calling me so late, Gobet?" he said in French.

I replied in his own language. "It's not Gobet."

"Who is this? Where is Gobet?"

"Gobet is sleeping like a little baby."

"Are you deaf? I just asked, who is this?"

"A man with a job to do, nothing more and nothing less."

There was a pause. "That's a long name, stranger. What do you want with me at this hour?"

"I want the safe return of Juliette Dupont. Immediately."

The phone went dead.

"What happened?" Michelle asked.

"They hung up."

"What did they say? Is Juliette all right?"

"We didn't get that far."

"So, what now?"

"We wait. They'll call back. They might be tracking the phone, depending on how much they trusted their man in there, on the sofa."

The phone rang.

"You miss me?" I said.

"Who am I talking to?"

"I already told you. I'm just a man with a job to do."

"And this job is something to do with Juliette Dupont?"

"At least you're not denying knowing her."

"I know her all right. We all know her. She has made a lot of people very angry, including me."

"That's too bad."

Out of nowhere, he said, "My boss will not return the girl."

"That's funny because right now I'm your boss and I'm telling you to return her."

"Oh yeah?"

"You either return her now, or I'll find you and punish you and then you'll return her. Your choice."

He exploded, raising his voice and ranting so hard I almost felt the spit coming through the phone. "You do not tell me what to do! You think you can just call me up in the middle of the night and make threats to me like this? To me? To Léon Diouf?"

I had learnt to be wary men who referred to themselves in the third person. They were often unstable and unpredictable.

"Yes, I do think I can do exactly that because that is what is happening right now. Where do I pick the girl up from?"

The rage phased into an unhinged laugh. "You really are something stranger. A special case. You are also a dead man, or should I say, a dead fool? I don't know how you got this phone, but when Gobet tracks you down he will cut your throat like a pig."

"Listen up, Diouf. Your man Gobet is decommissioned, so forget about him. And in my possession, I have the contents of his desktop on a couple of USB drives, including some very interesting documents pertaining to some of Europe's leading ladies and gentlemen. Politicians, bishops, business moguls, you name it. Some of them are more photogenic than others, but the internet doesn't judge."

A much longer pause. "You're bluffing."

"What can I tell you? Gobet sang like the proverbial canary. What if I tell you I know all about Operation Sirocco, or as I have renamed it, Operation Sicko?"

I heard a hand being passed over stubble. Another pause, a sigh. "What do you want?"

"I already told you. I want and fully expect the safe return of Juliette Dupont. When I see her alive and well, and she is in my safe custody, you will get the disgusting contents of Sirocco returned to you. If you come after Juliette after I have gone, I will consider it personal and you will not enjoy the last few hours of your life."

"I must talk with my superiors."

"Do that, but forget tracing the phone. For this reason, you call me back in five minutes with the answer or you're getting a bullet in your head before sunrise. I have one here with your name it and there's one for Max Vaillancourt as well. Yes, that's right. I know your boss's name, too."

The phone went dead a second time.

"So, Juliette is alive?" Michelle asked.

"I'm sure she is. We have all the best cards."

We finished the coffee and smoked another cigarette. The temperature dropped beside the river. Inside, Gobet was still in the same place on the sofa. I had deliberately left him in an uncomfortable position so when he came to he would have to move. No playing dead. That had not happened yet. Then the phone rang.

"Do we have a deal?" I asked.

"Is Gobet alive?"

"Just about."

Diouf said, "If you bring him and the USB drives to us, we will trade them for the girl's life."

"Where?"

"There is an abandoned building we can use not far from your current location. It is a disused abattoir. You can park up there and deliver Gobet and the USB drives to us. Be there in one hour."

"Make it two hours," I said.

"Very well." He gave me the directions.

"This is how it works," I said. "I will deliver Gobet and the USB drives to the abattoir in two hours. When I arrive, Juliette will be standing on her own. I will drive to her. She will get in the car. Gobet will get out of the car. He will have the USB drives. I will drive away from the abattoir with Juliette. If you fire on the car, I will shoot Gobet and you and then go and find a takeout burger. I will then find and kill your family before dawn."

"Be at the abattoir in two hours."

He cut the call.

Michelle shifted. "Do you really have to talk like that?"

"These are not nice men, Michelle. And they're not playing games."

She gave an unhappy nod. "Do you think we can trust them?"

"Of course not, that's why we're going now and getting there an hour early. That way we can check out the site in advance and get some advantage. Don't worry, Juliette's going to be fine. Right now, we have to get Gobet into his car and get on our way."

"Tell me you have a plan, Bill."

"Always."

TWENTY-NINE

Because he was unconscious, Gobet was deadweight. I walked him out of the study in a fireman's lift, down the outside steps and over to the rear of his car. I decided the Peugeot was ready for retirement and the Merc was more powerful and offered more comfort. Michelle ran ahead and opened the boot and I put him inside. Here, he started to come around, moaning and blinking in confusion just as I slammed the lid down and dusted my hands off.

"Will he be all right?" Michelle asked.

"Why, taking a shine to him?"

"You know what I mean. Can he breathe? I don't want to be responsible for someone's death. Not even his."

"You're not responsible for him, I am. And he'll be fine anyway. He'd die of starvation before he suffocated in there. We can try that later, but for now, let's go."

"Bill, that's not funny."

"I suppose not."

I drove us to the abattoir. We spoke very little in the car. I turned the radio on and I turned the radio off. I wound down the window and we smoked. The window went back up. It was very late night and the journey was mostly country lanes and the occasional roundabout. Village signs came and went in the flash of our headlights: Villeroy, Vinantes, Thieux. We passed few other vehicles. It was too late for traffic, even this close to the capital. More time passed. Michelle fell silent and when I turned to look at her across the broad transmission tunnel, I saw she had fallen asleep. Her head rolled back against the rest as she dozed, lulled by the soft hum of the big engine and the gentle blue glow of the dashboard lights. For a while, at least, she was free of the torment of worrying about her baby sister and what she might be enduring at the hands of men like Gobet.

When we reached our destination, I slowed down and took the turn off the road. The change in engine revs and speed woke Michelle, as did the juddering of the car as we progressed down what quickly became nothing more than a track, rutted from years of disrepair. She muttered something as she opened her eyes, and then stared out of the window. We had made it to the abattoir in good enough time to do what I wanted. Michelle was on autopilot and I was thinking about Diouf.

When we got there and pulled up right out the front, I realised we'd made the entire journey and I'd barely seen a mile of it. It was raining again, but light. The big single wiper swished intermittently back and forth on the windscreen as I peered out through the glass and checked out the place Diouf had selected as the rendezvous. I could see no sign of any cars, and we were still over an hour ahead of the designated meeting time, so I killed the engine. Then I had another thought. A better plan. Engine back on. I reversed the car back until I was at the abattoir end of the approach road and parked at a forty-five-degree angle, blocking any way forward into the abattoir's front yard.

"Are we there already?"

"You fell asleep."

"Why are we parked here on the approach road?"

"Because it forces Diouf to park up behind us. He can't get around us and the fields on either side of the road are fenced off. It means he can't get his vehicles up to the abattoir. We're setting the agenda."

She nodded. "Okay."

"Okay."

"And what a horrible place," she muttered. In the back, Gobet thumped and kicked and rocked the car from side to side. "He sounds angry."

"He can go to hell. C'mon. We need to look around the place before they arrive. You think Monsieur Gobet has a torch in the glovebox?"

She opened it up and pulled out a Maglite. "He's a very organized man."

"Then let's go and take a look," I said.

We climbed out of the car, and I walked around the back and opened the boot. I shone the Maglite at Gobet. He blinked and looked away, cursing behind his tape-up mouth. I grabbed him by his jacket and pulled him half up out of the boot. Like his hands, bound up behind his back, his legs were also bound together at the ankles and knees with construction tape. No amount of dexterity or determination would get him free. I grabbed his ankles and pulled them up over the edge of the boot. I pulled the knife from my pocket and he widened his eyes. I guess he didn't know where the blade was about to go and his imagination was running wild.

"I'm cutting the tape off your legs. Then you will get out of this car and stand up straight and still. The tape stays on your hands and mouth. If you make a move towards either of us or make a run for it, I'll shoot you down and leave your body where it falls. Do we have an understanding?"

He wasn't happy about it, but he gave a short nod.

"Then get out," I said. "We're going for a walk."

He did as I had instructed, but his eyes darted all over the place. I guess he was looking for a way out, a way over the fence and across the fields. But not only was his knee smashed, I'd already checked all that out and knew he had nowhere to go. More to the point, neither did Diouf when he turned up, no doubt mob-handed. Because of the angle I had pulled up at, Gobet's Merc was blocking the approach road completely. Diouf would have no choice but to park up right here and walk up.

Just like we did now. With blood strained jeans, Gobet was limping a few paces in front, with my gun trained on his back, Michelle was at my side. We didn't talk as we walked up to the old building. When we got there, I saw the abattoir was as advertised – old and abandoned and in terrible condition. Originally painted white, there was a lot of exposed brickwork and crumbling breezeblocks. I could just about make out the painted name of the former owner on the wall: Sauveterre. Even as slaughterhouses went, it was a bleak place. Junk from inside had been pulled out by thieves and vandals and strewn all over the broken tarmac out front. A metal staircase riddled with rust led up to the second floor. Where once had been a door, now a hole opened into darkness. I struggled to find one square metre not covered in graffiti.

We found an entrance and walked inside. The interior was even worse than the outside. Right in front of the door was an upturned skinning machine, also covered in rust and graffiti. Then, beyond this machine was a wide-open space. Concrete floor, high roof, narrow windows smashed out long ago. In the centre of the space was a carcass loader arm bolted to the floor, its bucket cylinder broken and hanging down like a snapped rib. Behind that, fixed to the wall was an evisceration platform, a bleeding elevator and some blood tanks. Above our heads, a steel monorail supported several industrial grade stainless steel hooks covered in thick cobwebs. This must have been the main processing line, once busy moving carcasses from one section to the other. A rank smell pervaded everything.

Diouf's kinda place.

But I was more interested in the layout, and after ordering Gobet to stand still out in the open where I could see him, I quickly reconnoitred the main floor and adjoining offices to get an idea of what was where and what could be used as cover if the worst came to the worst and an exchange of fire broke out.

I turned to Michelle. Gobet was too far away to hear us. "All right, the best place we can retreat to is behind the cattle-killing box over by the southern fire exit. Failing that, we go over there behind the blood dryer. It's further from an exit but it's better than being caught out in the open."

"How do you know what all these things are?"

"I'm a farmer's boy. This isn't my first time in an abattoir."

She nodded but said nothing. She was taking it all in, taking in exactly what happens in a place like this, in order for her to be able to live and eat the food she enjoys. It's always the same first reaction and the same sound in their voices. The hard reality of seeing a place of mass slaughter, the surgical equipment of death, each carefully designed for every specific task you can imagine. It didn't bother the farmer's boy, but the upmarket journalist from Paris looked mildly disgusted.

"Come on, we should go outside," I said. "I want to take a walk and get some fresh air. You look like you could do with some as well."

"Yes, but walk where?" She checked her watch. "Diouf will be here with my sister in a few moments."

I considered my reply carefully. Then, I went with honesty and said, "Your sister's not coming here tonight, Michelle."

She looked up at me sharply, her face contorting into a study of true anguish. "What do you mean she's not coming? The bastard Diouf said he would trade her for Gobet and the USB drives."

"That's not happening. Sorry."

"I don't understand."

"Like the animals raised for slaughter who came to this place, Diouf asked us to come here for one reason only and it wasn't to give us Juliette."

"He wants to kill us."

"Of course, but we have something he wants. Gobet and the USB drives."

She wasn't convinced. It didn't matter. We had a job to do and it was long past time to get it done.

I called over to Gobet. "All right, back outside. We're going to have a look around the back."

THIRTY

After we'd checked out the rear yard, I was satisfied Diouf could only approach from the front. There was a side entrance he couldn't see from the front, but that was it. After ordering Gobet to stand in the middle of the abattoir where I could see him, just behind the main entrance, I set us up in a good position behind one of the cranes and a large, rusted offal hanger. Behind us, a fire exit provided a good exit should we need it, but only to the yard. Then it was a climb over a wall. I'd already tipped an offal trolley upside down and pushed it up against the wall to facilitate a way over it. This did not work in reverse, allowing anyone in, and it was the best I could do in such a short time.

From our position inside, I was able to see right across the building and out through the main doors into the front yard, past the Merc and down the approach road. We had some spare time, so I synchronised the GPS tracker to an iCloud account and took a few seconds to think things through. Rehearsing an action like this pays dividends if you have the time. But we didn't have to wait long until we saw the flash of main beams on the treetops as a car turned off the B road and pulled into the approach road. It was closely followed by a second vehicle. When they drew closer and parked up behind the Merc, we could see what sort of vehicles they were. A white Renault Koleos in front and a black Jeep Cherokee behind it.

"You think this is Diouf?" Michelle asked.

"I don't think anyone else is driving out here at this time of night."

"No. It was a stupid question."

The doors opened and some men climbed out. Boots crunching in the detritus laying over the old tarmac. One of them switched on a torch and swept the beam over the Merc and around the car park and then over the abattoir's façade. The beam streamed inside and flashed in our eyes.

"Get down," I said.

When the beam had passed, Michelle craned her neck to see around the base of the offal hanger. She gave a long, weary sigh. She sounded tired and afraid and disappointed.

"I told you not to expect Juliette."

"I know, but still, one hopes."

I saw one of them pull out a handgun. He called out to us. "If you're here, show yourself, stranger."

They talked in rapid French. The speed of their words and their accent made it difficult to understand what they had said. I asked Michelle. She leaned into me. "They say they're getting the girl out of the Jeep, Bill. Juliette!"

I didn't think so. "Just take it easy. It's not your sister." I rummaged around in my pocket and grabbed the magnetic GPS tracker I'd got from Bonzo. I handed it to her. "Listen carefully. When I tell you, I want you to go back into the courtyard through the side entrance, over the wall and go across the field back to the B-road. Then you keep low and stay tucked into the hedge and crouch-walk back up the approach road until you reach where their cars are parked. When you get there, you need to put this GSPS tracker underneath Diouf's car. That's the white Renault. Can you do that?"

She shook her head. "No way. I'll get caught."

"You won't get caught."

"Why not?"

"Because I'll be shooting at them the whole time. They'll fan out and advance towards my position. No one will expect you to be approaching from the rear. I need you to do this for me, Michelle. Juliette needs you to do it."

"I don't know..."

Outside, one of Diouf's men opened the rear door of the Jeep and hauled someone out into the night. It was a woman and her hands were tied behind her back, but they had placed a black bag over her head. This reinforced my doubts that they had brought Juliette Dupont out here tonight.

"That's Juliette!" Michelle said. "I recognize her clothes.

That's her jacket, Bill. You were wrong. They brought her here."

"I wasn't wrong."

"All we have to do is give them Gobet and the USB drives and they'll send her over to us."

"It's not Juliette, Michelle. She's too valuable to them."

She shook her head again, face scrunching up with cognitive dissonance. She wanted it to be Juliette so much, the hope had flooded her better judgement out of her mind. "I don't understand, why would they…"

"It's someone else," I said quietly. "Hence the bag. If they take off the bag and it's Juliette, I'll buy you and your sister a three-course meal at the hotel of your choice when all this is over."

"But it has to be her," she said, the tone of her voice already betraying her doubts. "It just has to be."

I had no chance to respond. A man I presumed was Diouf strolled out into the middle of the front yard and raised his voice.

"We brought your woman, stranger. Now give us Gobet and the flash drives. I'll count to ten and if I don't see Gobet, then I shoot her in the back of the head."

Michelle gasped. She looked like she was going to be sick. I pressed the GPS into her hand and locked my eyes on hers. "It's not her, Michelle. We find her by tracking Diouf when he leaves here."

"With Gobet?"

I gave her a look. "Gobet's not leaving here tonight, either."

She was disgusted. "I can't take any more of this. I might have been a cop once, but now I'm just a journalist, Bill. I'm just a writer."

"When I say go, you get that GPS on the white Renault. Think of Juliette and stay the hell out of their sight. Do not let anyone see you, Michelle. Not a soul. They'll kill you in a heartbeat. You understand?"

Her eyes were filling with tears.

"Juliette needs you to do this."

She nodded. "I understand. When you say go, I go."

I nodded and called out through the entrance at Diouf. "Take the bag off the woman's head, Diouf."

There was a short silence, and then the men outside laughed. To them, this was all nothing but a game. Anyone who controls the rules of anything always thinks it's a game. Pretty soon, they would lose control and I would start making the rules. Then it wouldn't be a game anymore. As they laughed, one of them leaned into the back of the Jeep and pulled out four compact machine pistols. MP5s. This got my attention. He handed them around to Diouf and the other men.

"What's the matter, stranger?" Diouf called back. "You don't trust us."

I raised my phone and zoomed in on his face, snapping a picture of him. My thought was maybe passing it to Sparrowhawk in case I needed some more information. "No. It's your face. You don't have a trustworthy face."

The laughter stopped. Diouf called out, "Show me Gobet, or she dies right now. I've been more than generous and you have had more than a count to ten."

"You heard him, Gobet," I said. "Take a few steps into the fresh air, son. Make a break for it, and you've got some lead in between your shoulder blades."

Gobet never looked back. He took a single tentative step forward, and then speeded up into a slow walk. He was just a silhouette from my perspective. When he reached the threshold, I ordered him to stop and stand where he was.

"The USB drives are in my pocket, Diouf," I called out. "But if I don't see the woman's face, I'm putting a bullet in Gobet and I'm out of here with all the evidence. You won't catch me. You and your men are all too fat."

Anger flashed across Diouf's face. He was a man unaccustomed to being insulted in front of his men.

"You want to see her face?" As he called out, he pushed the woman forward a few steps. He and his men all came away from the vehicles and approached the abattoir's main entrance. They were maybe thirty yards from Gobet. The woman was a little closer.

I said, "Let's get on with it, Diouf. I don't have all night."

I turned to Michelle. "Go now. Away to the north and then down through the field, keeping low and behind the hedge. Hit the main road, turn left and creep back along the approach road, hugging the shadows, just like I told you. There'll be an explosion. Ignore it. You'll be safe. Just deliver the GPS and then you go back to the main road and hide somewhere. This is about to kick off."

She took another look at the woman with the bag on her head. "Are you sure it's not my sister?"

"Totally sure."

She was still unconvinced. Truth was, it could have been Juliette, but I thought it very unlikely. Diouf was too arrogant and had too much confidence in himself. He'd spent his life bluffing vulnerable people into submission. Tonight, all that changed.

I watched Michelle slip out through the side door and disappear into the yard. She was on her own now. I wouldn't see her again, or know if she had been successful until this was all over. Outside, Diouf pushed the woman closer and ordered Gobet to come outside. Gobet had been trained well. He was staying put until I told him what to do. I waited a few seconds and figured Michelle was almost down at the B road by now. It was time to draw them further away from the vehicles and give them something else to think about. I kicked things off by firing a shot into the back of Gobet's head and killing him where he stood.

THIRTY-ONE

He slumped to the floor, dead. The sound of the shot was still echoing in the night when I fired on the black Jeep's gas tank and ignited the fuel inside. The tank exploded in a ferocious fireball and blasted the vehicle's windows out in a thousand shards. As pieces of plastic and car seats and belts and buckles and other assorted junk rained down on the front yard, Diouf and his men were frozen for a second, taking in the simultaneous sight of Gobet's dead body and the burning wreck of the Cherokee. It had all happened so fast. But then they finally jumped into action.

Diouf ordered them forward at angles to break my line of fire. I'd expected this, but I was shocked when Diouf padded forwards to the abattoir, raising his gun as he passed the terrified woman with the bag on her head and shooting her through the bag three times. She too fell down dead, a few yards from Gobet, coming to rest in a pile of burning detritus ejected from the wreck of the Jeep by the explosion.

As I prayed that I'd been right about Diouf not bringing Juliette, he and his men streamed into the abattoir through the main entrance. I fired on them, killing two on the spot. That left Diouf and two others. I could have taken out all three of them as they ran for the cover of one of the meat hangers, but then I'd have no one to track back to Juliette and the trail would be cold. I had to do this the hard way. I was already crouch-walking along behind the crane and heading over to another position, having given my old one away. As Diouf and his two men concentrated their fire on my old position, I made my way over to the other side of the abattoir and fired again. These were not well-trained men. They broke up and spread out. I aimed my gun at one of them who had settled behind an old breaking saw on a metal table, directly beneath a skylight, allowing a faint light from above to brush the top of his head. I fired and killed him. It was too easy.

But Diouf wasn't stupid. He had sent the other guy around to attack from behind me and the first I knew of it was when I heard him shuffling somewhere off to my seven o'clock. I spun around to see him lunging towards me, a combat knife in his hand. He knocked the gun from my hand and it clattered on the concrete floor. Now I was unarmed, so looked around fast for something to use against him. I grabbed a pneumatic rib bone-breaking saw that had been lying on a leg-cutting machine. It was long-past working, but the rusty blade was intact and made a good, improvised weapon.

He glanced at the saw but never hesitated, slashing the combat knife in my face and missing my nose by inches. I raised the saw and thrust it forward, embedding the rusty, circular blade in his chest. He cried out in agony and fell back into the dust. He reached up and grabbed the adjustable handle and wrenched the blade out of his body with a hoarse scream. I was already running over to my gun. I snatched it up and fired. I hadn't counted the rounds out and this time I was out of luck. When I squeezed the trigger, I heard nothing but a series of hollow, dry clicks. I was out of ammo.

The man was bleeding heavily. Behind us, I heard Diouf call out and ask what was going on over there in the shadows.

"Bastard tried to kill me with a saw, Léon..." he mumbled.

I spun the gun in my hand and rammed the grip into his face. Unlike the plastic grip on Manu's Beretta, the Glock's metal scratched over his chin and cheek and nose like a cheese grater, tearing the surface layer off and making him howl in pain. Unluckily, my aim was a little off and I failed to knock him out with a solid blow. The gun slid right off his face and I followed it, arm outstretched, leaving my right flank vulnerable.

He exploited the error savagely and planted a hefty cross into my ribcage. The blow was almost enough to break a rib, or maybe more than one rib. As it happens, I got away with a severe bruise and enough time to step away from him, just missing the sequel. In this case, the sequel was a switchblade he pulled from his pocket and rammed into me, aiming for my stomach. Thanks to my sidestep and the blood pouring from his wounded chest, he missed and tumbled forward, losing his balance. He got to his feet once last time and ran towards me, having recovered from the blow on his temple, but the other wound was too great. He looked about as angry and full of revenge as you would imagine him. Eyes wide-open, bared teeth, blood all over his face from the deep cut I had delivered above his left eye and a growl on his lips.

I lifted the Glock up above my head and brought it crashing down on the crown of his head, knocking him out with a thin papery splitting sound. He went down hard, cracking his forehead on the corner of a stainless-steel washbasin and hitting the filthy concrete floor beneath it, never to rise again.

You pays your money and takes your chances.

I reached down and grabbed the switchblade from the dead man's hand. In the other hand, I continued to wield the inverted Glock like a knuckleduster and made my way through the shadows towards Diouf.

"You're next, fat man," I called out. "If you count that sack of crap Gobet, that's five down and one to go."

But Diouf was already gone. I watched him bobbing out of the abattoir, handgun at his side. At the entrance, he twisted his substantial frame around and fired off a few more rounds blindly into the inside of the building and then vanished into the front yard. I broke cover and made my way across the abattoir until reaching the entrance. Here, I watched him run past Gobet's Merc and fumble at the door of the Renault. I was grateful he'd lacked the presence of mind to shoot out the Merc's tyres, but I'd counted on him being too rattled to think straight after watching his entire gang getting killed right in front of his eyes. That had paid off. As he fired up the engine, conducted a sloppy three-point turn and raced away down the approach road, I prayed once again Michelle had managed to place the GPS.

When I saw his back lights turn onto the B road and move out of sight, I stuffed the Glock into my barn coat and walked over to the woman with the bag on her head. I had told Michelle to stay down at the B road for two reasons. One was for her safety. This was the second. I pulled the bag off the woman's head and looked closely at her face. It was not Michelle's sister. I blew out a long breath and thanked my instinct. Finding a woman to pose as Juliette Dupont would not be hard for a man like Diouf. In the circles he moved in, it would be only too easy to threaten some poor girl they'd snatched from somewhere. Blackmail her, beat her, threaten to harm her family. I didn't know who this woman was, but I draped the bag gently back over her head and gave a silent prayer for her. It was all I could do. The authorities would find her family if she had any, and maybe they could lay her to rest.

But seeing her dead eyes had stirred something inside me.

Now, more than ever, I wanted to lay Diouf to rest.

And everyone else he was in business with.

THIRTY-TWO

I climbed into Gobet's Merc, cruised around the burning wreck of the Jeep and made my way back down the approach road. I was able to pass it because they had parked straight, parallel to the road. I had blocked the road by parking the big Merc at an oblique angle. At the end of the approach road, I pulled up and stepped out of the car. I called out for Michelle. After a few seconds, I saw movement in the hedgerow on the far side of the road. She clambered out, brushing leaves and twigs from her jacket and hair and stumbling on her heels as she ran across the road to me.

Before opening the door, she stared into my eyes, wide-eyed with terror. "Was it Juliette?"

I shook my head. "No. It was someone else."

She said nothing and climbed into the car. When I slid in beside her, I saw she was crying. I closed my door and started driving.

"I take it you delivered the GPS to Diouf's Renault?" I said.

She nodded. "Yes. For Juliette."

By the end of the road, I found a side road and pulled over into a small forest. I took out my phone and started the next phase of the mission.

Michelle leaned over the partition between the two front seats and watched desperately as I navigated to the right place on my phone.

"Can you see it?" she asked. "Can you see Diouf?

"Not yet. Be patient."

I entered my password and navigated to my iCloud account. I thumbed through to the location services and easily found the GPS signal. I'd had to hope they hadn't searched the vehicle, including underneath it, for a tracking device and tossed it aside. But there were no problems. Michelle had attached it to the base of the car during the fire fight and there was no reason for Diouf to be suspicious or consider he might have been compromised in some way. But, there was still time for him to become suspicious and search the Renault. Time would tell. If we were good, we were good. If we got rumbled, another plan would be in order.

"What if they find the tracker?" Michelle asked. As she watched the little red pulse on the screen, she'd had the same thought as me. She'd said 'they' because she hadn't realised I'd killed them all except Diouf.

"We'll be fine." I handed her my phone with a smile. "And no stalking me when all this is over. I'll change my password, anyway."

She smiled, the first time in hours. "I promise."

"Now we get moving. We're tracking a vehicle, not a person. If he changes car or parks up and walks, we're at another dead end."

"I can't believe you're doing all this for me, Bill. I don't even really know you."

I fired up the ignition and we reversed out of the small forest. "Don't take that too personally. No one knows me. It's just the way it is."

"Why is that, I wonder?"

I spun the wheel and reversed the car onto the sealed B-road. Turning the wheel again, I engaged the automatic transmission into Drive gear and we started our pursuit of the bugged car. After a long silence, Michelle spoke again.

"I asked you why that might be? That no one knows you, I mean."

I didn't know how to answer. I don't like talking about myself. "It's always been that way. I grew up on a farm, no brothers and sisters, my mother died when I was a young boy. It was just me and Dad. He was a good man, but a busy man. Most farmers are busy men. Raising livestock is a hard business. He worked twelve-hour days in the winter, sixteen-hour days in the summer. We drifted in and out of each other's lives. I spent a lot of time alone, especially out in the woods on our farmland. I learnt to trap and hunt. And I played truant."

"What does that mean?"

"Skipping school. I played up. Broke some laws. Got into trouble. That put even more distance between me and Dad. He couldn't understand it because he worked so hard. He was an honest man. Then again, he had a mother and a brother. That was a big difference between him and me and he knew that difference, but what could he do? Then I joined the army and passed P Company."

"I don't know what that is either."

"It's a selection course for the Parachute Regiment. I liked the sense of family they provided. As long as you pull your weight and do your bit, it's a close-knit place. I felt like I belonged somewhere for the first time in my life. Good blokes, in the main, but I moved on for a new challenge."

"So you are not still with the Parachute Regiment today?"

"Not anymore, no."

"That's right. You said you were retired. But what did you do next?"

She had no business knowing about my time in the Regiment. She was a journalist after all, and so was her sister. And she knew my real name. I kept things simple. "This and that. If you want the short story, the army didn't work out either."

"So what do you do now?"

This was a good question. The truthful answer was

impossible to find. “I’m just looking for answers, Michelle. I’m going to keep using up tarmac until I find some place to settle down and then just mind my own business.”

“If you’re trying to stay out of trouble, I don’t think you’re very good at it.”

I smiled briefly. “You could say that. Trouble has always had a way of finding me, no matter what I do. I don’t know why that is.”

After half a mile of silence, she said, “Why were you so certain they would not bring Juliette here tonight?”

“People like Gobet and Diouf are as predictable as snakes. Easy.”

“None of this is easy, not for me. I just want her back, safe. Then I can put all this behind me.”

We drove a mile or so well behind Diouf’s car for twenty minutes, out of sight and following the signal on the phone. Then it deviated from the B-road and pulled onto the main road heading into the east of the city. I wasn’t familiar at all with the countryside here, but I knew enough about Paris to build a good mental picture of where he was driving and how we could stay on his tail while remaining out of sight. It was after midnight now and well into the small hours. I had already convinced myself that I could return Juliette safely to Michelle and the rest of their family, but that wasn't the big problem. The big problem was tying things up so Diouf and his masters wouldn’t come after the Duponts after I had moved on. Men like that lived for revenge and I knew Michelle's family would most certainly not be safe unless the account was settled fully. Anyway, that was the big problem. Subsidiary problems included evading Quartermain and getting to Virkler on time.

As for the big problem, I had learnt long ago not to climb inside the minds of men like Gobet or Diouf. Once inside a place like that, there was no getting back out again. Their mental landscape was a bleak place of selfish animal desire and greed and they tolerated no obstacles. These men were the thieves and murderers and serial abusers of our world. There was no talking to them. No negotiation. Never any stopping them. They never learnt, they never changed. They were never persuaded. In a way, all this made my big problem much easier to solve. If I left any loose strings, I knew Michelle and Juliette would be dead within days, there could be little doubt. This meant there was only one way to solve the big problem, and that was the hard way. The hard way for them, not me.

In the corner of my eye, I saw Michelle turn to me in the darkness of the car. "Do you think they will hurt Juliette after what happened tonight? Now that Gobet is dead and we have nothing to trade?"

"I don't see why. They lured us out here to kill us both and put an end to what was becoming a major thorn in their side. They screwed that up. Gobet means nothing to them.

If anything, Juliette is now even more valuable to them because they need her more than ever as a bargaining chip. They'll try and play a similar hand to the business they tried and pulled back at the abattoir, and for that they need her. It's what we need that bothers me more."

"I don't understand."

"We're going to need more weapons than I thought. More firepower."

"What do you mean?"

"I thought a few handguns would do the trick, but that all changed when I saw Diouf's thugs handing MP5s around like candy canes at a Christmas party. If a grubby little low-level toerag like Diouf has kit like that, imagine the hardware the real big boys have. I'm talking about Max Vaillancourt. We can keep an eye on where Diouf goes via the tracking app. We won't lose him, but we need to get back into the city and have another chat with Bonzo. Men like Diouf and Vaillancourt love the fight when the fight's not fair, so now it's time to even the playing field a little bit."

With my words still hanging in the air, I stared out at the road and settled down for the short drive back to Paris.

THIRTY-THREE

I drove the car, lost in my thoughts. It was late, and the other headlights shone in my eyes as we made our way towards the city. The traffic was still light. Rain came and went. The Merc cruised nicely. I thought about the night I shot Mulgrave and Operation Taipan. About Quartermain hunting me down. I wondered who the hell Sparrowhawk was and why he was helping me, and more about why he thought I could help him. That bothered me, and while he had been trustworthy up to this point, that meant little. Lulling someone into a false sense of security in this way was a trick as old as the hills. I was still a long way from fully trusting Sparrowhawk. I considered Matthew Firebrace, Mulgrave's replacement and whose side he was on, but I didn't even know how many sides there were. I knew one thing. If Firebrace was on my side, it would make my life a lot easier, because as a Lieutenant-Colonel in the SAS and a senior figure at D19, I was too high up the greasy pole to be left alone as a loose cannon on deck.

I checked my watch and other problems drifted into my

mind. Like Virkler. He was out there somewhere right now, in this city, cursing my name. Too bad. Louis Virkler could wait. Michelle had seen me check my watch. She craned her head forward and looked into my eyes.

"Supposed to be somewhere else?"

"Wherever I am, I'm supposed to be right there."

She looked at my smile and returned it. "Sounds a little too philosophical for this time of night."

She was probably right. For the rest of the journey, we drove in silence. Occasionally, she would look at the GPS signal on my phone, wedged in Gobet's mobile phone holder beside the steering wheel. It looked like Diouf was heading deeper into the city. That was good news. We had to go back into Paris to get the extra gear from Bonzo, so this made my night a lot easier. But nothing goes to plan. We pulled up in the same place we'd used before, near the Café de la Paix, and walked to Bonzo's house, but as soon as I turned the corner of the street, I knew something was wrong. The front door was wide open, which was something Bonzo would never do. I drew the Glock and told Michelle to get behind me.

"What has happened here?" she asked.

The desperation and fear in her voice were a perfect match for my mood. "I don't know, but it's not good. Bonzo would never leave his door open like this, not even for a second. You wait here."

I stepped inside the door, gun raised into the aim and made a quick sweep of the two front rooms. In the one on the right, I saw Martina. Her dead body was sprawled out on the floor, halfway towards a table with a telephone on it. It looked like she was trying to call for help when someone had shot her in the back. There was no sign of Gustav, their Alsatian. I looked away and stepped back out into the hall, closing the door gently behind me.

"Don't go in there," I said.

"Why not? What happened?"

"Martina's dead."

She gasped. "My God..."

"Stay behind me."

Making my way along the hallway to the kitchen at the back, I saw Bonzo's legs protruding from under the dining table we had eaten at just hours before. I stepped over to him, the Glock's muzzle still held high and made sure the room was clear before dropping to my knees and pulling him out from under the table.

"He's gone, Bill..."

His voice was weak, tired. He was very badly beaten. I'd seen a lot of damage in my time, but I knew as soon as I saw him that he'd lost the sight in his left eye. He'd also need some false teeth when they rebuilt his lower jaw, which was horribly smashed and swollen. It was going to take a lot of time and money to get my friend his face back. But then I saw the stomach wound. A bullet wound. The Harley-Davidson t-shirt was ripped open to reveal charred flesh encircling a gaping, bloody hole. In the intense pain, he had curled up under the table at the end of a short trail of blood smearing the black and white tiled floor.

I crouched down on my haunches and reached out, laying a hand on his arm. "You look like shit, Bonzo."

He flinched and mumbled something. As he spoke, Michelle took a tentative step into the kitchen.

"What was that?" I asked. "You're not speaking clearly. Have you been drinking or something, you mad old bastard?"

He tried to laugh. "She stormed out, Bill. Me and Martina had a blazing row not long after you left. About something so stupid. About the damned washing up. Crazy." He laughed, but it turned into a cough and he had to pause to get some control of his breathing back. "We had this massive ripper of a row and she stormed out. Said she was staying with her friend for the night. That's when he came, seconds after she left." He stared me in the eyes. "I was in here washing up. Listening to Aerosmith. Rocking out and singing along and this bastard walks right in here as if he owns the place. Holding a shitty old Glock like the one I gave you, fitted with a sodding suppressor. She was lucky to get out before he turned up, old son. If she'd been here, he would have killed her, Bill. Killed her stone dead. Talk about luck."

"You're right," I said, fighting the image I had seen back in the front room. There was no sense telling him the truth. He wouldn't survive the hour. "She was lucky to get out."

"He took my phone and cut the landline to stop me from warning you," he said, coughing. "I've just been lying here waiting to die, old son."

"It's okay," Michelle said, visibly disgusted by his wounds. "It's all right. Take it easy."

More mumbling.

"Who did this?" I asked, although I already had a good guess.

"It must be Diouf's men," Michelle said. "The bastards! How many were there?"

Bonzo shook his head. "No, not French, not a gang... he was alone. English. You know, don't you, Billy boy."

"Quartermain."

He nodded. "The one and only."

"What did he say?"

"He told me I kept some very bad company and what a treasonous bastard you were. He said..."

He started coughing up blood. Michelle fumbled in her bag for a handkerchief and gave it to me.

As I dabbed at his mouth, I asked him what else Quartermain had said.

"He said you are next. He said he will kill you. That he is

always watching you. He told me you drank two bottles of Stella Artois in the Café de la Paix this evening. That you were with a woman. He described Michelle. She spoke to a man outside. That the only reason he didn't kill you then was because of witnesses. He's following you. Cat and mouse, old son. It's cat and mouse. He said you will be dead before the next sunrise."

"Who is this man, Bill?" Michelle asked.

I ignored her and ran a hand through my hair and sighed. Taking another look at the wound, I wondered if maybe Bonzo might make it after all. It was worth a shot. "All right, first we need an ambulance. Right now. After that, we can talk about the man who did this."

Her voice flared a little. "I asked who this Quartermain man is, Bill. Look at what he did tonight!"

"He's someone who doesn't like me very much. We'll talk about it later."

"Fine. You can tell me all about it when Bonzo is safe." She got out her phone and began to dial. "I will call an ambulance before it's too late."

But it was already too late. He was dead. When I gently closed his eyes with my hand, Michelle was silent for a few seconds and then ended the call and put the phone back in her pocket.

"What now?" she said at last.

"Another name just got added to the list," I said through

gritted teeth.

"What list?" she asked, the frustration rising in her voice.

"You don't want to know. Let's get some gear and move out. Juliette needs us more than ever."

THIRTY-FOUR

The GPS signal on Diouf's Renault had been stationary for the entire time we'd been at Bonzo's place. It was still in the same place as we climbed back into the Merc and that place was Pigalle. This bordered the 9th and 18th arrondissements, north of the river, and was notorious for the sex shops and adult peep shows it hosted on its boulevards. With the help of Michelle's knowledge of the city, it didn't take us long to get up there and we were soon cruising past the famous red windmill, the Moulin Rouge. It was too late for the cabaret to be open, even here, but the district was still humming with activity.

Michelle looked quietly through the window as we closed in on the GPS signal. I said nothing either but watched the neon signs streak past in the rain. Drifting along with the night, I was startled when my phone rang. The caller ID was blank but I answered it all the same.

"This is Blake," I said quietly. "Go ahead."

"Not best pleased to hear about Freddy Butler, Blake."

Sparrowhawk.

I said, "Word seems to travel very fast these days."

"I have very good friends in Paris, Colonel. I thought we'd established that."

"So it seems."

"Let's be realistic. Butler was one of the biggest arms dealers in Western Europe and a former inside man. One of ours. You realize we do keep an eye on people like that from time to time?"

"He was a good friend of mine, Sparrowhawk. Mind your manners when you talk about him."

"You can expect nothing less from an educated chap like me, Blake. *De mortuis, nil nisi bonum dicendum est* and all that."

Of the dead, nothing but good is to be said.

"Then let's keep to that, Sparrowhawk. I'd hate to have to wring your neck and defeather you."

"Steady, Blake. Let's keep things civil."

Michelle lit a cigarette and offered me one. I declined.

"Who do you mean when you use the word 'we', Sparrowhawk?"

"You know I can't answer that."

"In that case, maybe you can answer this. Why are you calling me?"

"A good question. The answer is, I want to know why you're driving through Pigalle."

"We've already established that you can track my phone.

I'm not impressed. I could have stopped that a long time ago if I'd wanted."

"But why Pigalle?"

"Because I have a lead here."

Out of nowhere, he said, "Quartermain killed Butler."

Michelle's head turned.

"Bonzo already told me that. He still had a few seconds of life in him when I got to his place. Quartermain also murdered his girlfriend. A Slovakian named Martina."

"I mean Quartermain's involvement is officially confirmed. He already called it in. My understanding is that you're next and he's closing in on you fast."

"You have a location?"

"Not at my fingertips. He's good at slipping off the radar. I might be able to ask a friend of a friend."

"He seems very fast at tracking my movements down. You have my phone details. I still wonder if you're passing him my location."

"You cut me deep, Bill. And after all we've been through together, too."

"Why are you helping me, Sparrowhawk?"

A long silence. "I'll answer that by telling you my real name. Would you like to know my real name, Bill?"

"If it really is your real name, then yes. But you can spare us both the time that would be wasted by you telling me a fake name, if you please."

"My name is Richard Bentinck."

I felt my blood run cold. "I see. Then, you're related to Michael Bentinck by some degree."

"A rather close degree as a matter of fact. He was my brother until Mulgrave had him killed. Now, another chance to win a prize. Who did Sir Michael Mulgrave employ to strangle my brother to death?"

"Jack Quartermain."

"You're every bit as bright as they say, Bill. As bright as a shiny brass button."

"And you're keeping me alive tonight in return for killing Quartermain."

"The shiniest brass button in the whole, wide world."

Things were starting to make sense. Michael Bentinck was a former SIS officer who had helped me back in London when Mulgrave, the Foreign Secretary had tried to frame me and my boss Peter Brookline for the murder of a Russian double agent posing as a diplomat named Natalia Zakharova. It all got very messy. Bullets started flying and I went on the run. Mulgrave had told me personally that he'd had Bentinck murdered alongside several other good men, including another agent named Wainwright. I never knew Bentinck was strangled and I never knew Quartermain had done the wetwork.

"I'm sorry, Richard. Michael helped me. I think he probably saved my life. He gave me the name of a man named Wainwright as a contact, and this led me to a good friend of mine named John Grant. I guess I would be dead and buried if it weren't for your brother."

Every inch the upper-class Englishman, just like his brother, Richard Bentinck showed not the slightest glimmer of weakness or vulnerability. "I'm glad he was of help to you in your hour of need, Bill. He was a good man. Perhaps now you understand why I'm rather keen on not only stopping Jack Quartermain from killing another innocent man, which in this case is to say you, but that I also harbour certain dark fantasies involving his untimely demise. I'm an intelligence man, Bill. So was Mike. People like us look at facts. We analyze data subsets. Listen to fragments of conversations snatched from stolen mobile phone signals. When things get muddy, we don't have the right footwear."

"And this is where I come in, right?"

"Right."

"Keep talking."

THIRTY-FIVE

Sparrowhawk continued, "Everyone in the SIS knows about D19. It's unofficial, but we all know about it. We all knew about Brigadier Brookline. He was a sound man. We also all know about Colonel Blake. I've read your file. I've looked at your psychological profile report. I just told you that is what I do for a living. I'm highly trained and respected. It's what I'm good at. And I know a chap like you doesn't like to blow his own trumpet."

Michelle was still smoking. She looked at me now, confused. She hadn't understood the trumpet thing. Come to think of it, it was kind of a stupid turn of phrase.

"I'm not a killer-for-hire, Richard. Any killing I've done was always sanctioned by Her Majesty's Government."

He laughed, but it was a sad, bitter sound reflecting a broken man. "I'm no hero, Bill. I can't do this myself and yet Quartermain must die. He must. *So cowards fight when they can fly no further; So doves do peck the falcon's piercing talons; So desperate thieves, all hopeless of their lives, Breathe out invectives 'gainst the officers.*"

"Latin quotes and Shakespeare all in one night. You're bringing out the big guns."

"A little Henry VI never hurt anyone, Bill."

"From the quality of the conversation, I'm guessing you're an Old Blue like your brother."

"Yes, I went to Christ's Hospital. My brother and I were well-educated."

Christ's Hospital was a British public school, which meant it was a fee-charging private school. The terminology was a quirk of history. Established in 1552, it was originally started as a charity school, also called a blue coat school, with the mission of giving children from poorer backgrounds a higher quality education. But 1552 was a long time ago. Edward VI was on the throne. Today, many of the pupils are the children of serving military personnel. I know this because I served with some Old Blues in the Paras and also D19. Whether I ever met any in the SAS or not is my business.

"Well, I'm a farmer's boy, Richard. I grew up on the land and went to a very ordinary college."

"You think there's a cultural divide between us?"

"If you're asking me to kill another man simply to avenge your own brother's murder, then I think maybe there is."

A longer silence. I signalled to turn off Rue Blanche and turned east onto Rue le Bruyère. While I was talking to Richard Bentinck, I'd been keeping an eye on the GPS signal. It looked like Diouf had certainly settled down for the night because the car still hadn't moved since we'd arrived at Bonzo's place.

"Are you still there, Richard?"

The roads were growing narrower. We were heading back into the darker quarters of Paris again. I cruised past a *Pharmacie*, identified by a green neon cross lighting the drizzly night. The scent of Michelle's cigarette drifted past my nose. I turned to her and indicated that I would like one of my own. She rummaged around in her bag and handed me one, then lit it for me with her silver lighter. The Merc's turbocharged diesel engine purred like a satisfied tiger as we rolled effortlessly through Saint-Georges towards our destination.

"I'm still here, Bill."

"I'm going to kill Quartermain, Richard, but not because of your brother. I'm going to kill him because he shot Freddy Butler to death and murdered Martina."

"I understand."

"Good. I'm not a gun for hire. I'm not a thug or a psychopath."

"That's the second time you've told me that."

I noticed we had turned into Diouf's road, or at least the road where his car was parked. "I'm not here to be psychoanalyzed. Have you got a location on Quartermain yet?"

"Still no. Last known location was Butler's residence. After that, he went dark."

"Because Freddy Butler kept his mouth shut. He was a good man. He could have told Quartermain about what I was doing in Paris tonight. That would have given him a lead, some names. He'd have got closer to me, and faster, too. I owe Bonzo my life, but Quartermain will pay for his murder with his life. That's how things are going to shake out."

I pulled the car over to the side of the road a few hundred yards away from the white Renault.

"I'm pleased to hear it. I'll get you his whereabouts as soon as I can. When you find him, give the bastard a bullet from Mike, please."

"We'll see. But there's something you can do for me right now."

"Anything for a friend."

"As you will doubtless know by now, I'm sitting outside a residential apartment block in Pigalle. This is because I'm tracking a man called Léon Diouf. I suspect he's got a woman up there somewhere. Maybe a wife. I don't know and I don't care. Thing is, it's a big block. Now you have a name and a location, is it possible to get a specific apartment number?"

"I'll see what I can do. Hold the line."

It went quiet. In under a minute, he came back. "There

is a woman named Refka Diouf living in an apartment in the block you're sitting outside."

He gave me the details and I thanked him. Then, I cut the call. After I smacked a fresh magazine into the Glock, all courtesy of Bonzo Butler, I stuffed it down into my barn coat pocket and quietened down for a few seconds. Thought it through. Things were coming to a head.

THIRTY-SIX

We stared at the white Renault for a short while. Diouf's Renault. It was parked up on the side of the road in a bay reserved for residents. I had pulled over further back to be on the safe side, but now I drove forward a little closer and rolled to a stop outside a shabby Tabac on the corner of the road. For a few seconds, Michelle took some time out from worrying about her sister and reminisced about her teenage years in the area as we had navigated the backstreets. I had made use of the time to dissuade her from coming into the apartment with me. She had objected on the grounds of her police experience but eventually gave way to my argument. Truth was, she hadn't been a detective for many years, she hadn't fired a weapon before and we had no backup. If things went pear-shaped inside the apartment, I was pretty sure I could get myself out of any kind of trouble Diouf could serve up, but protecting Michelle might prove problematic.

I cut the engine and pushed back into the seat.

"You're sure you want to go in alone?" she asked.

"Yes. Very sure. Where did you put the GPS tracker?"

She told me. I glanced at the clock on the dash. "I won't be long. Wait here."

I climbed out of the car and walked along the pavement until I reached the white Renault. I scanned the area and made sure no one was looking, then I reached under the car and retrieved the GPS tracker. I put it in my pocket and gave the Glock in my other pocket a reassuring tap. Then I made my way towards the building. Back in the sixties, Le Corbusier turned a lot of Paris into concrete. Brutalist and uninviting, many of these places today were old, broken-down and covered in graffiti. Diouf's place was older and more upmarket, but still a little shabby, especially for Pigalle. But it seemed to fit in with the area. The twilight zone between Pigalle and the bottom of the hill at Montmartre was mostly safe but had a reputation for occasional danger.

It was on these very streets that *Les Apaches*, a violent gang of criminals and thieves and killers roamed looking for victims during the Belle Époque era, or what English speakers might call late Victorian to Edwardian era. The Apaches were notorious for slitting the throats of unsuspecting people, including tourists. Nothing like that happened here today, but it was always worth being aware of your surroundings and their history. There were still young men trying to be Apaches on these streets, looking for trouble and mugging people for drugs money.

I approached Diouf's building, a tall seven-storey place with a flat roof. Music blared from various windows. At least three of the streetlights were out, and the one directly in front of the block was flickering. I drew closer, hands in my pockets and head tucked down into my chest. Collar up and trying to look like I walked this way every night. I heard men arguing in Arabic and then someone screamed at them in French to shut up or he'd call the cops. The Arabs laughed. A loose dog ran across the road ahead of me and disappeared into the night behind the apartment building and I continued on my way.

I reached the entrance and looked up. Diouf's place was on the seventh floor. Each floor was separated from the next by a square of concrete and soot-streaked cladding representing where the stairwell was turning for the next storey above. I walked inside and decided to take the lift. I recalled it and stepped into a thick stench of urine. Even though it was behind a steel mesh, the security camera had been smashed to pieces. I selected the top floor and rode up on my own. The lift arrived and the doors creaked open. The light in the corridor was also flickering and a persistent bass thump was emanating from an apartment to my right. I made a note of the door to the stairwell and then made my way along the corridor to Apartment 4. I rang the bell.

When the door opened, a face jutted out into the corridor. It was a woman of north African appearance. Black eye and split lip, both fresh. I stepped closer, drawing my gun and pushing the muzzle into her stomach and forcing her back into the apartment with my other hand, kicking the door shut behind me with my boot. That took less than five seconds and I was in Chez Diouf. The place was underlit and smelt of incense and burnt vegetables.

"Don't make a sound," I said in French. "Not one single sound, all right?"

She nodded, terrified. I closed the door.

"Who else is in here?"

She widened her eyes, terrified. She tried to talk but nothing came out. I grabbed a fistful of her blouse and pushed her back down the passageway into the living room, scanning all the time in adjacent rooms for any sign of Diouf. All rooms behind me were empty. When we got into the living room, a small space with a static bike in the corner and vintage *Job* advertising posters on the wall, I released the fistful of her blouse and pushed her down into a chair and checked the room behind me. Also empty. Swinging the gun back into her face and putting my fingers to my lips to indicate silence, I walked across the room and checked another spare bedroom and then the bathroom. Nothing. I walked back into the main room.

"Where is the man who was just in here?"

Eric Clapton was singing *I Shot the Sheriff* on the stereo. It was too loud, but I let it play in case she decided to scream.

"There was a man in here a few minutes ago. Drives a new white Renault. Where is he now?"

"You mean Léon. My husband."

"If you say so. I want to know where he is."

"Let me guess, he owes you money. He owes everyone money. He gambles, you see."

"I asked where is he?"

"He left a few moments ago. Why?"

"It doesn't matter why. I want to know his location, now."

"As I said, he just left."

"Not in the lift."

"He used the stairs, and so would you if you lived here. When it's not breaking down, it's a great place to get mugged and it stinks."

"Down the stairs," I said, repeating her words and peering out of her window. No sign of him. "Where is he going tonight, so late?"

She clearly did not like Léon very much and gave him up easily. "He sees a *putain* down in Saint-Denis. A woman from Marseille called Estelle. He thinks I am so stupid I don't know, but I know."

"Description?"

"Thin, white, dark hair. Thirty-five years old. Estelle Simon. Looks like a whore."

"Where exactly does she work?"

"Rue Saint-Denis, at the *deuxième* end."

"The second arrondissement?"

She looked me up and down and smirked. "Maybe you have been there, hein?"

"How is he travelling there? His car is outside this building."

"He has another car he uses whenever he visits her. A silver Citroën. He uses it in case he gets caught and fined. The white Renault is mine."

"What's the Citroën's registration number?"

She gave me the number. "You've been a lot of help. Send anyone down there after me and I'll be back before dawn. I'm much nastier at that time of day."

She said nothing and I walked away, stopping in the hall to turn around. "Nice posters, by the way."

Then I left, leaving the door open. I went back to the lift and called it up. Two young men of Maghrebi descent stepped out of the noisy apartment and wandered over, hoods over their heads, and started to wait for the lift. They looked like the kind of guys Parisians sometimes called *banlieusards*, or in English, the closest translation is joy riders. As it turned out, they were no trouble. We got inside the lift and rode it back down to the ground floor. I'd had my hand on the Glock in case there were any nasty surprises with the young lads or maybe something else out in the lobby. Never know. The doors creaked open but the lobby was empty and the two teenagers stepped ahead of me with their hands in their pockets and went their own way.

I walked back to the car and found a nervous Michelle waiting for me.

"You were gone a while," she said. "I saw some dangerous-looking guys come out and thought maybe you'd been hurt."

"I'm fine." I climbed into the car and slammed the door, locking it and putting on my belt. I started the engine. "You want the good news or the bad news?"

"Bad news, always."

"Our man wasn't in there."

"Damn it."

"But the good news is we know where he is. Sounds like he regularly visits a prostitute in Saint-Denis, called Estelle Simon. Mrs Diouf was only too happy to give us a lead."

"You believe her?"

"I don't have a lot of choices, but yes, as it happens. She had a look of revenge in her eyes and a face full of black eyes and split lips courtesy of Léon's bad temper. My guess is this was a good chance for her to get some of her own back against her old man. We need to go and find this Estelle woman. Then we'll find Juliette."

THIRTY-SEVEN

When Estelle Simon stepped into the dim light of the back streets of Saint-Denis, she looked ten years older than thirty-five. Her face was partially obscured by an old umbrella but it was possible to see some detail. Dyed blonde hair with dark roots, fringe cut low to obscure eyes ringed with heavy makeup. Dark red lips, almost black in the streetlight and long dark nails covered in chipped polish at the tips of cold white fingers. She wore a faded denim jacket with the collar turned up and a tight leather skirt at the top of two long legs hidden behind black glossy tights. All of this was perched on a pair of three-inch stiletto heels and wrapped inside a cloud of cheap perfume.

"A couple," she said. "Interesting."

"We just want information," I said.

She looked disappointed. "I don't sell information."

"You will for what I'm paying," I said, getting out my wallet.

She pursed her lips, eyes all over the leather wallet. "How much are you willing to pay?" She spoke fast, in Marseille

French. I found it hard to catch every word, but Michelle had no problems.

"Fifty euros," said Michelle. "It's important."

Estelle gave a sour laugh. "Pfft."

"One hundred euros."

She turned to leave. "Whatever you want to know, this is not a serious offer. I have work to do."

Michelle fumbled in her bag for her purse. "Five hundred euros! Please."

"This must be important," Estelle said.

"It's about a kidnapped woman," I said. "And the people who took her."

"Kidnapping?" Estelle turned in the rain. "Non. They will kill me if they find out I spoke to you."

"Please," Michelle said, taking off her watch. "You can have this. It's real gold."

Estelle took the watch. "It's a start. But I will need cash, too. Enough to go home at the very least. To leave Paris and never come back. These are very dangerous men."

"Then you know who we're talking about?" Michelle asked.

"One thousand euros," I said. "And not a cent more. You can catch a train to the south with that and rent a room out of the way somewhere until you work out what to do. If it really is home, you'll have friends there."

She slid the watch on and considered it. "But cash or I

walk."

I opened my wallet, revealing several crisp one hundred-euro notes. "You get nothing until we have the information we need."

She sniffed, lowered the umbrella and stared up into the drizzle for a few moments. It coated her face and made her mascara run. I wondered if she was high on something. Then, she came back down to Earth, brought the umbrella back up and nodded. "All right. We have a deal. What do you want to know?"

"You know this man?" I showed her the picture of Diouf I had snapped on my phone back at the abattoir. When she saw his face, she visibly recoiled in disgust. It wasn't subtle. "Oui, I know this man. He is a pig."

"Did you see him tonight?" Michelle asked.

She hesitated.

"We know you did," I said.

"Then why ask?"

"Please, we need your help. When did you see him last?"

"Briefly, and less than an hour ago. He came to ask me if I wanted to go to a party in the south. In Marseille. He knows it's my hometown. He said he wanted me there because the women at the parties were ugly. He wanted my company."

"Your company?" Michelle asked. "As in your paid company?"

Estelle sucked her teeth and scowled at her. She twirled the umbrella, spraying water out in an arc. "His exact words were, *il n'y a jamais que des thons à ces choses.*"

Des thons. I was confused and turned to Michelle. "Tuna?"

"An insult for ugly women," she said.

A car drove past and the driver honked the horn. Estelle waved at him and he vanished in the night.

I turned away from the car and looked at Estelle. "And what did you tell him about going to his party?"

"Are you crazy? I told him no. That I have work to do. These parties last all night and well into the day. I haven't got that sort of time to waste unless he pays and he said he would not pay. As I say, I told him no. If he didn't like my answer, he could go and talk to my boss about it. Serge. Everyone is afraid of Serge. No one argues with Serge, so Léon went away again. Besides, I've been to those parties before. They're not the sort of place a good person chooses to attend, believe me."

"Why not?" I asked.

She gave me a weary look. "Why do you think? You must know what I'm talking about if you are on the trail of a man like Léon Diouf. He is scum and so are his friends. And he spends time with some very powerful people. Really big scum if you know what I'm saying. They are the ugly ones, not the women they abuse."

She lit a cigarette and exhaled smoke from under her umbrella. It drifted up into the rain like a thin mist.

"You have any names?" I asked. "I mean, names of the people who go to these parties?"

She tipped her head. "But these names are very expensive."

Michelle sighed. "Listen, don't make me angry. We need your help."

"Oui, mais… this is a service economy. You want help, you pay for it."

"How much for the names?" I asked.

"I'll sell you the biggest name of all for one thousand euros."

Michelle gasped and turned to me. "She's lying. She's on the make. We can't waste time here anymore. We should go."

I was already counting the ten one-hundred euro notes out into my hand in front of Estelle. "Give me the name and I'll give you the money."

"Yeah, right. Or maybe, I give you the name and you give me a slap and walk away, hein?"

"Five now, five after the name."

She grudgingly consented. And after taking possession of five of the notes, she said, "Nicolas Duris."

Michelle frowned. "Are you certain?"

"You can have confirmation when the rest of the money

is in my hand."

I handed it over.

"Not only have I seen Duris at these parties, but he is also a regular. A central figure, you might say."

"You mentioned that name to me earlier," I said to Michelle.

"Yes. Nicolas Duris is the EU Commissioner for Trade. So, yes. He's important."

"And vile," Estelle said.

"Are you sure about Duris?" I asked. "Think before answering, Estelle, because I know where you work and I'm not afraid of Serge."

"I just told you it was Duris and it was Duris. He is at the party now. With Max Vaillancourt, one of his private security associates. Dangerous people."

Estelle might have been lying, but I didn't think so. That meant this was the breakthrough we were looking for. Nicolas Duris was a high-ranking member of the European political elite and his presence at sex parties involving trafficked women had just been confirmed by someone who had been at those parties and personally witnessed him there.

Michelle fumbled with her wallet and pulled out the photograph of her sister that she had shown me back at the station. "Have you seen this woman?"

Estelle frowned and stood on tiptoes to peer inside my wallet.

"I have no more money, Estelle," I said, showing her my empty wallet.

"But this is important," Michelle said. "We think Diouf and his gang kidnapped her."

Estelle looked at the picture and shrugged. "Maybe." She took another drag on the cigarette.

Michelle visibly deflated. "Please look again. This woman is my sister. Her name is Juliette Dupont."

Estelle's eyes widened. "Then yes. I saw her with Léon tonight. They are taking her down to the villa for the party in Marseille. Then he is taking her to Africa. They never come back from Africa."

With the picture in her hand, Michelle turned and walked away. She was distraught.

"Last question," I said. "Do you know exactly where this party is happening in Marseille?"

She nodded. "Max Vaillancourt owns a villa in Petit Nice. Vallon de la Baudille. Duris is a regular guest there."

"You know where that is, Michelle?" I called over.

She was standing with her back to me, face up to the rain. "Yes. On the Corniche in the 7th arrondissement. Right on the water. Big money."

Estelle laughed. "Vaillancourt is a millionaire. And Duris is a millionaire, too, and not from his little political salary. The money comes from trafficking, mostly via bribes and blackmail. Welcome to the real world."

"Thanks, Estelle," I said. Stuffing my empty wallet in my pocket. "You might have saved a woman's life tonight."

"I'll remember it forever," she said, her voice heavy with sarcasm.

I walked over to Michelle. "Let's go and get Juliette."

We stepped over to the car. Michelle got in and I walked around to the driver's door. I opened the door and Estelle called out to me from under her umbrella.

"Hey, mister! You think anyone is going to save my life anytime?"

I said nothing and climbed inside the car. Door closed and the central locking on. Turned the key and fired up the engine. Heater on. Radio on low and pulled away, leaving Estelle and the streets of Saint-Denis in the rear-view mirror behind us.

"You think we can get to her before they take her to Africa?" Michelle asked quietly.

"I can't promise that, but I'll do what I can."

THIRTY-EIGHT

As we drove south to Provence, we said almost nothing to each other. I just stared into the darkness and enjoyed the smooth ride provided by the expensive Mercedes, but Gobet's CD collection left a lot to be desired. I opted for a radio channel, some kind of talk show with occasional light jazz. Sullen stuff, downbeat. It matched the mood. It seemed to tune Michelle out, too. She was sitting quietly now, listening to the music and soft chatter, eyes fixed in a thousand-yard stare somewhere off to our right. Maybe she was looking at the rain, maybe the passing cars. I never asked.

I didn't know what she was looking at, but I knew what she was thinking about. Her sister. She was thinking about Juliette and if we were going to be able to track her down and save her. When Estelle Simon had identified Nicolas Duris, she had registered the news with serious shock on her face. She had already had a run-in with Duris that had cost her everything, including her police career. I felt the same, but for me, it wasn't personal. Tonight, Michelle Dupont had learned that not only had her sister been right about everything, but that she was now a victim of it. I understood how hard this must have been for Michelle to process. She felt small and powerless and disgusted.

In the quiet hum of the engine, we relaxed and cruised effortlessly along. Michelle turned to me and reached out with her hand. "Thanks, again. For everything you're doing. I still can't believe how much help you've given me. You don't know me or my sister. I'll never forget it. I'll be forever grateful, even if we can't save her. Thank you, from my heart."

"Forget about it. Let's just get the job done."

"And if we get the job done, what will you do?"

It was a good question. I was unsure about the political situation in Britain. I'd shot Mulgrave and killed him back on his family estate. His replacement, Firebrace, hadn't indicated whether or not I was considered a *persona non grata* back in England or not. I'd heard D19 had been shut down. I'd heard it was up and running. I had no home. To top it all off, before I shot him, Mulgrave activated a protocol called *Taipan*, branding me the highest-level domestic terrorist and placing me under what was essentially an irrevocable death sentence. The assassin, Jack Quartermain had already murdered Freddy Butler and his girlfriend Martina and, according to Sparrowhawk, aka Richard Bentinck, he was closing in on me, too. I had another loose end to tie up in the form of Louis Virkler, but I had to get Quartermain off my back first, if possible. Appreciating that Michelle didn't need to know any of this, and probably wouldn't want to know any of it after what she had been through tonight, I gave her the most honest answer I could find.

"I'll probably stay on the road for a bit longer."

"In France."

I shook my head. "Not in France, not even in Europe. I need to go somewhere much further away and say goodbye to someone I once loved very much."

"Who?" she asked, turning to face me, her eyes suddenly full of interest. "Where? You realize I know almost nothing about you except your father was a farmer."

"I can't tell you who or where Michelle. It would put us both in danger. Right now, you're safe. You know nothing, and I need to keep it that way. If you know anything about me at all, especially where I'm going, then your life will be at risk."

She was shocked. I saw that. She hadn't thought about any of this.

"You mean, this terrible Quartermain man?"

I nodded once. "But you're safe from him right now."

"But what about when you leave? Will he come after me?"

"No, I'm not going to let that happen. I'll make sure he

knows where I'm going. I'll leave him a trail of breadcrumbs. I know how to do that. I can make sure he leaves you alone by giving him another conduit of information. It's just like channelling water."

"I don't understand any of this anymore. It all frightens me. I just want me and my sister to be safe again and live normal lives. That is all."

"And what about that?" I asked, changing the subject. "What will you do when all this is over?"

"I know what I want to do. I want to buy a vineyard in the Loire. I am going to make wine. No more cities, no more crime, no more journalism and no more politics. I will ask Juliette to go in with me. I know after this nightmare she will walk away from her old life and join me. It will be a better life."

"Sounds good to me."

The conversation burned out. We smoked, she fell asleep. I thought a lot about that vineyard in the Loire and what a great idea it was. I also thought about leaving a line of breadcrumbs behind me to pull Quartermain away from Michelle and set him up for some kind of final showdown. I knew where to start putting down the crumbs, but had to give one more push to finding Juliette Dupont. If Estelle had been telling the truth about transporting her to Africa after Vaillancourt's party, I knew that would end any hope of ever finding her again. If she went into Africa, I would have to walk away from both the Dupont sisters.

The drive was long and quiet. Miles slid past us as fast as minutes. Tarmac growled under the Merc's fat, expensive tyres. We were driving south across France and towards the dawn. The sun finally crested over the horizon. Long, flat rays of weak light the colour of cream brushed across deep, rolling fallow fields just off to our left. My father told me once that French fields were longer and slimmer than English ones because of their ancient inheritance laws demanding each son got an equal piece of land. Maybe that's true. I never checked it. Sounds plausible, and he would know.

Dad worked the land all his life, out in the sticks of Oxfordshire. My childhood memories are a mix of long, hot summers and deep, frozen winters. The smell of cow muck, horseflies and wildflowers. The touch of high tensile rusty barbed wire wrapped in rolls behind the barn. Up before dawn to break the ice on the troughs. Sneaking the old man's whisky and climbing up onto the barn roof to drink it in under the stars. Tractors. Abattoirs. Livestock auctions. Quotas, tax, accountants. The time we had to sell good land to a property developer to stay afloat. Good times but hard times.

I lit a cigarette and took a long drag and let my mind do the walking. It wandered further down memory lane and that was all right with me. It took me by the hand and walked me right back to the day of my first hunt. Man has always hunted. I was brought up to see hunting as just another part of life, an important part of the year's cycle. One of the ways my father made money on the farm was by holding various hunts throughout the year. Letting the local hunt use the land for a fee. Terms like hedge-hopping, billet and cold line were all part of the vocabulary of my youth. Depending on the season, people came from far and wide, sometimes from abroad, to hunt hares or foxes and sometimes shoot wildfowl.

My first hunt. Not even a teenager and I thought it would be a good idea to give the fox a helping hand. I was no sab but something about it got on my nerves. Just something about watching the hunters gathering outside the farmhouse in their scarlet coats and white winter breeches and plaid cubbing coats. That's not how Dad dressed. When I remember him, I see him wearing his old, torn wax jacket and muddy jeans, a hole in the right knee. Herringbone cloth cap that had seen better days. Working clothes. Not like the man in the bright yellow canary vest sitting high on his warmblood breed, making a fuss and trying to shepherd the other riders into place.

There are many different ways you can disrupt a fox hunt. You can take control of the hounds with a huntsman's horn. You can get out in front of the hounds and stop them by cracking a hunting whip. You can spray citronella. It masks the fox's scent and breaks the line the hounds are following. You can do lots of other things. That day, I ran out into the woods with an old huntsman's horn and blew it to drag the hounds away from the fox, which I'd seen running to a burrow I knew it used out in the woods. It ended the hunt that day and made some very rich people very angry.

Dad never knew I'd done it. If he had, he'd have hit the roof.

I drifted back to the drive. The night had been long and hard and we were both ready for sleep and yet now it was dawn. Rest would have to wait. As the sun rose higher above the horizon, we finally crossed into Provence. After the long drive, I turned off the main road and followed the regular GPS towards Vaillancourt's place. As the automatic transmission moved down into second gear for the junction, the revs changed and snapped Michelle out of her thoughts. She looked at me and whispered something quietly to herself, something I never caught. I indicated right. Estelle had been very clear about Vaillancourt's parties going through the night and lasting into the day. She said they sometimes lasted several days. It was pure luck, a stroke of serendipity, but arriving around dawn was probably the best time. Everyone at the party would be burned out after the night, hungover, tired and most likely sleeping.

That was always a good time to put a door in.

THIRTY-NINE

I checked the Glock was loaded with a full magazine, stuffed two hand grenades into my jacket pockets, and shouldered the MP5. I thought about Bonzo's murder as I got tooled up. I'd got the gear and a few other things from his place back in Paris and the memory of his dying breath was hard to put away. I climbed out into the street and told Michelle to wait in the car. She was getting used to that by now. We'd parked up at the bottom of the hill on Marseille's Corniche, an impressive stretch of luxury properties stretching along the waterline at the western edge of the city's 7th arrondissement. Looking back, I should have parked further away to keep her safe, but hindsight's fifty-fifty.

The gear I was carrying was light enough to let me move around a bit sharpish, but also more than enough to take out whatever security Max Vaillancourt cloaked himself and his political masters in. If they were like any other close protection firm, I doubted they'd be carrying anything more than semi-automatic pistols and a few spare magazines of ego, but after seeing Diouf's MP5s, they might have been kitted out with something more substantial.

I made my way up a narrow cobblestone lane and approached the property. White plaster walls maybe twelve feet high on either side of the lane draped in vines and bougainvillaea. The south was warmer and we had a clear sky. The early sun reflected on the white stucco walls of the mansions stacked up on the hill behind Vaillancourt's villa. The building itself was three floors high and covered in ornamental balconies bursting with fan palms and bright red geraniums. I needed to see more, so I shimmied my way awkwardly up a cypress growing next to his rear wall and observed a large and carefully manicured garden of olives and rosemary and lavender bushes, all neatly placed around the centrepiece, a large oval swimming pool. It was a beautiful place concealing ugly secrets from an unsuspecting world. I was about to put an end to all that.

As for people, I only saw a fat guy asleep in his trunks on a seahorse-shaped lilo lounger in the middle of the pool and a young woman in a bikini with a towel half-draped over her, also asleep beside the pool in a hammock strung up between two young umbrella pines. The house behind them was quiet except for the low pulse of a bass beat coming from what appeared to be the ground floor. Most of the lights were off. I counted several cars parked outside a shuttered garage block, one of which was a silver Citroën. I was willing to bet the family farm it belonged to Léon Diouf. As I scanned the property for locations of doors, windows and gates, a man in a silk dressing gown stepped out onto a wooden deck area and looked up at the sky and smiled. He was holding a steaming cup of coffee, which he now smelled and sipped from and smiled again. I didn't know who this man was, but he was not Nicolas Duris.

The coffee drinker turned around and stepped back inside the kitchen. That was good with me. The other two sleeping off last night in the garden were still both fast asleep, so I climbed up over the wall and lowered myself down the other side behind a head-high rosemary bush. My boots crunched down on some woodchip mulch, but not loud enough to wake them. Also good with me. In the shadows of the rosemary, I fitted a suppressor into the Glock's muzzle. Most Glocks are not suppressor-ready, but I'd picked up a specially-designed attachment back at Bonzo's. I could hear him now, in my mind, laughing and telling me this was just another reason I should have taken the SIG. It clicked into place and the job was done. I glanced up at the house. No one in sight.

Out of the shadows and through the border, my jeans brushing against the shrubs. I stepped out onto the patio and walked around the pool and towards the house. I considered taking out the two sleepers but rejected it. There were few ethical considerations about sparing them. These were people who had attended a party involving trafficked women. They got lucky because I didn't want to blow two rounds on a couple of semi-naked hangover victims when I was still unsure about what and who was inside the villa.

They slept like babies as I walked past them and moved casually up the steps and across the decking towards the kitchen door. Right hand, a suppressed Glock. Over my right shoulder, a submachine gun. Two fragmentation grenades in my pockets. If I'm being honest, thoughts of Freddy Butler and Martina were right at the front of my mind, even ahead of Juliette Dupont. Use whatever motivates.

Coffee guy was sitting at a table, steaming mug right in front of him. His eyes were closed as he savoured the smell of the roasted Java beans. He had a satisfied expression on his face. His silk dressing gown was monogrammed. MV. I guessed it was Vaillancourt unless someone else was wearing the gown. Then again, I just did not give a damn who it was. When my shadow fell over his face, he opened his eyes and smiled at me. Silhouetted in the back door, I was hard to make out. I knew that.

"That was one hell of a night," he said, shaking his head. "And this is one hell of a morning, Max."

For a few seconds, he thought I was a guest at the party. He squinted at me, confused. "I don't remember you from last night. Who are you?"

"Your judge, jury and executioner."

Then he saw the guns and tried to stumble back out of the chair and make a run for it. The first round went into his head and two more in the heart. Three muted thuds, sounding like I'd fired through a pillow and he crashed back off the chair and hit the deck.

I was already gone, through an internal door on the other side of the kitchen and into the villa. First thing I saw was that Vaillancourt was right. It had been one hell of a night. A few people were crashed out in chairs. Full ashtrays everywhere, empty vodka bottles all over the floor. Curtains half-drawn, dull light. The room stank of nothing good. On a smoked glass coffee table were a few lines of coke and a professional bong. I realised that the music I'd heard from outside and thought was coming from the ground floor was coming from some kind of basement.

Memories of Amzazi's trafficking hub back in Barbès-Rochechouart flooded back to me.

I looked around for an entrance in the obvious places and found one under a grand, sweeping staircase twisting up to the top floors. The door was locked, but not for long. There are many ways to pick a lock, but one of the fastest is to blast a nine-mil rimless tapered firearm cartridge into it. The lock burst apart in a shower of sparks and splintered woods. Before the dust settled, I opened the door and stepped inside, slow and calm. I lowered my gun and aimed down the stairs. I saw the hint of some dim lights and the music was much louder now. I checked no one was behind me and made my way down the steps.

I was heading into the wolf's lair.

FORTY

I reached the bottom and found myself in a small anteroom, painted black, one naked light bulb hanging from the ceiling. This was the dim light I had seen. Forty watts. The air was cool and dry like inside a game larder. This brought back memories from my childhood on the family farm. I saw another light, a strip of light at foot level. It was light coming from under a door. A door leading to the room with the music. I heard laughing and screaming at the same time. These guys really liked basements. It made my skin crawl. Instinct drove me to holster the Glock and get the MP5 off my shoulder. Whatever was behind that door needed terminating as fast as technology could deliver. I made my way over to it, stopping halfway to smash the lightbulb out with the stock of the MP5, plunging the anteroom into darkness.

I took a breath and raised my leg, putting the door in with my boot. It smacked out of the way in another shower of dust and wood splinters, swinging back hard and smacking with force against the inside wall off to my right.

The room was lit low and the first thing I saw was a huddle of men and women who had been standing around in a small, intimate huddle in front of a sofa in the centre of the room. Not like Amzazi's friends, these people were well-dressed. They had their backs to me, but when the door went in, they turned and gawped. Some were smoking, others held drinks, all caught off-guard. Two things flashed through my mind. The first was that I had found Léon Diouf. He was standing off to the right beside another door with a can of beer in his hand. That settled me these were the people I'd been looking for. The second was that none of them was Juliette Dupont. Then Diouf reached for a weapon in a shoulder holster. A woman saw my gun, screamed and dropped her glass. She was also well-dressed and professional.

This had to end fast, so I opened fire, cutting down all of them in a few short, bloody seconds. The rounds tore into their bodies, tearing flesh and chipping bone and exploding the glasses and cans in their hands. Empty cases flicked out of the MP5's ejector port and clattered to the floor near my boots and the gun roared and rattled until they were all dead.

Job done. No time to pause. I moved into the room and swung the gun up into the aim, sweeping the muzzle in an arc until I was satisfied the place was clear. It was. The music was still pulsing hard. I fired a short burst of rounds into the stereo and ended the noise. Then I stepped over Diouf's dead body and walked towards the other door. Whoever was in there knew someone was out here shooting. You couldn't fail to hear an MP5 unloading rounds into half a dozen people in the next room. It wasn't something you didn't notice. This meant they had advance warning.

I approached the door. It swung open, surprising me. A man was standing inside with a Steyr machine pistol. Someone else standing off to his left had opened the door. It was a coordinated move. Guy in the door opened fire with the Steyr, spraying the room I was standing in with fire. I dived for the cover provided by the wall to the right of the door, bringing my gun up and preparing to fire. Another burst of rounds and the ferocious sound of bullets tearing through the plaster. They were firing through the wall I was using for cover. I hit the deck and rolled out into the room, aiming for the sofa. I reached the new cover position fast and leapt up to my haunches and rotated my upper body and raised the MP5 and let them have it.

The gun exploded in my hands, releasing a dozen rounds into the man, almost cutting him in half. He collapsed to the floor, releasing the Steyr as he died. Mayhem everywhere. Others moving behind him. Another woman screamed. I heard a man shouting for someone to close the door. I recognized faces. The Italian Minister of Justice, whose name I couldn't recall. He was another one I'd seen with Mulgrave. And a man from inside MI5. Mawson was his name. Judging by the look on his face, he'd recognized me too. I had no time to think about what I was taking in. Things moved fast. As the herd scattered, I saw Nicolas Duris, naked from the waist up, reaching out for a shirt. Blood on his torso. Whose blood? The guy with the Steyr had dropped fast. It seemed unlikely that blood from the exit wounds would have hit Duris considering where he had been standing at the time. Duris yelled again, asking where the hell Max Vaillancourt was. It was Duris who had screamed at someone to close the door. I recognized the voice now.

I opened fire again, emptying the magazine and killing the man who tried to close the door. I was still squatting on haunches, but now sprung up and pulled the Glock out in one fluid move, firing another burst of suppressed rounds into the room as I advanced into it. The bullets buried themselves in a neat line in the plaster of the far wall to the left of Duris. Behind me, a man ran into the room I had just been using. I grabbed a grenade from the barn coat, pulled the pin and rolled it under the sofa in front of him. I took immediate cover behind the wall of the second room, raising my gun to kill Duris at the same time. The grenade's explosive force was terrific inside the confined space and blew the gunman into chunks. A cloud of blood, body parts, broken furniture and splintered wood and dust blew through the open door with high force.

Ahead of me, Duris had slipped out of sight, behind the angle of the door. I couldn't see him any longer. A woman screamed, asking him what the hell was going on. Still no sign of Juliette. I burst into the next room and took in a hell scene. Dead bodies, blood. A dead woman I had not killed. A scene of confusion given extra disorientation by a swinging ceiling light. The Italian politicians and Mawson were both long gone. I saw Duris heading towards another door. I raised the Glock and fired into his back. The bullets exited through his chest in a spray of blood and he fell to the floor in a heap. I moved forward, looking down at his corpse. Somewhere around now I made a mistake and dropped my guard. The first and last I knew about it was someone striking the back of my head. The impact was hard and swift and extinguished my consciousness in a heartbeat.

FORTY-ONE

When I woke, I guessed around an hour had passed. It just felt like that. I felt concrete on my cheek so I knew I was on the floor, and presumably still in the basement somewhere. Maybe a different room. It smelled damp and musty. The place was like a rabbit warren. They'd taken the MP5 and the Glock and the spare mags and the remaining grenade. That was to be expected. They were busy people. Duris had a lot going on in this place, and none of it was good. The scale of the operation was dawning on me. Trafficking all over Europe, Africa and the Middle East. Maybe Asia too. A dungeon in the home of Max Vaillancourt, one of Duris's close associates. But both Duris and Vaillancourt were now dead. Duris was confirmed, Vaillancourt was an educated guess. That was something, at least, but I was still in the belly of the beast, Juliette was still missing and Michelle was now isolated. I pushed myself up on my elbow and blew out a long, deep breath. It really had been one hell of a night.

Then I heard a voice. A woman thanking God in the darkness. Her voice was weak and pathetic.

"You're awake," she said. "Dieu merci."

I squinted in the gloom. It was hard to make her out because the only light was coming from a gap under the door. "Juliette?"

She moved her head back in surprise at the unexpected sound of her name, spoken by me in the darkness. "Yes… you know who I am?"

"If you're Juliette Dupont, then yes I do."

Her confusion grew. "But how?"

"I'm working with your sister, Michelle. We've been looking for you since yesterday afternoon."

"Mimi," she said distantly. "Is she safe?"

"I think so. I left her in a car parked up on the Corniche. Told her to get the hell out of Dodge if she thought she was in danger. I also told her to drive away and give up on both of us if she didn't see us by noon." I checked my watch. "Two hours to go."

"You shouldn't have come here," she said after a heavy pause. "Now you will die too. Perhaps they will find Michelle and the rest of our family. These people are animals."

"I worked that out all by myself. I'm Blake by the way. Bill Blake."

"You are crazy, Bill Blake. But thank you. I can't believe anyone would come into a place like this to rescue me. There is nothing here but pure evil. No one gets out."

"We'll see about that."

She was quiet again. Then she said, "I think I heard them killing someone. A woman."

I thought about the dead woman I had seen upstairs. After a long pause, I said, "Have they hurt you?"

She shook her head defiantly. "Not yet, apart from the kidnapping and the slaps and beatings and the black eye. They told me the serious stuff comes when I get to Africa. There is a warlord there who pays a lot of money for French women. It's one of the most lucrative parts of their trade, that and bringing African women into Europe. The whole thing is vile, and now I'm in the middle of it. I have been such a fool."

"You were trying to help these women."

"Duris is a top politician. At the very top. There's talk of him running for the French presidency. If you think he'll let us get out of here alive, then you're even crazier than I thought."

"Nicolas Duris is dead."

Her eyes darted over to me, the glimmer of hope starting to sparkle there. "What do you mean?"

"He's dead, Juliette."

"Are you sure?"

"Pretty sure. I put thirteen nine-mil rounds into his back. You don't come back from that."

For a long time, she didn't know what to say. Finally, she

said, "I don't believe it. He's so powerful. He's famous. He's…"

"Lying in a pool of his blood with a hundred grams of lead in him."

"My God. Did you kill everyone up there?"

"No, and what I just told you is the good news."

"What's the bad news?"

"Duris wasn't the only public face up there. I also saw the Italian Minister of Justice and someone from inside British Intelligence up there, too."

"Wait, Lorenzo Rossi is at the party, too?"

I clicked my fingers. "That's the bugger's name. That was bothering me. But yeah, Rossi is here too. I think he might have got away."

"I didn't know he was involved in all this. Another one to put in my exposé. If I survive this nightmare."

"You'll survive."

"How can you be so sure?"

"Instinct. Tell me something, Juliette, and this is important. Are there any other trafficked women in this house today?"

She shook her head. "I'm the only one. I heard them talking. They moved the others out at midnight and there are no more coming in until later today. A new batch from Africa going up into Europe."

A key in a lock. The door swung open and two silhouettes

stood above us.

"Get up."

Juliette obeyed immediately. Just a few hours with these guys had turned her into Pavlov's dog.

"What's it worth?" I said.

The man on the left pulled a gun. "Your life. Get up."

I got up off the ground and straightened up to my full height, several inches above both of them.

"Now, you get your hands up. Both of you. And step out here."

We stepped out of the room and into a corridor. One of the men was holding what looked an awful lot like my MP5, presumably reloaded with the fresh mag they'd taken off me. A Sonic Youth poster was on the door of the room we had been contained in. "Monsieur Vaillancourt certainly has rather rococo taste in music for a stuffed suit."

"Huh?"

I leaned into him. "I said, Max Vaillancourt has unusual taste in music for an old, perverted bastard."

He told me to shut up, but I was already too close. I shoulder-barged the guy with my MP5, twisted the weapon from his hands, pushed Juliette back inside the room and fired on the other guy. It was a short, controlled burst of three rounds, but enough to tear his throat to pieces. With the jugular severed, the blood poured out and his blood pressure dropped like a rock. He slumped down and was dead before he hit the floor. The other guy was behind me, fumbling for another weapon. I quickly saw that was also my Glock. I guess this bloke had taken them as trophies. I raked him with rounds from the MP5 and took the Glock from his shaking hands as he bled out on the floor.

Juliette was screaming. I took hold of her arm and shushed her.

"We're out of here, now. Keep it down."

She nodded but was horrified and trembling as we stepped over the two dead men.

"Where are we going?" she asked.

"I saw a garage outside. If my sense of direction is good, and it is, it should be accessible down the end of this corridor. We're going to take a car, find Michelle and get the hell out of here while we still can. Whoever ordered these two men to come and get us will already be missing our company."

FORTY-TWO

My sense of direction never lets me down, and this time was no exception. When we reached the garage, I quickly scanned the surroundings. It was more like a luxury car showroom, five berths wide. A Lamborghini Huracan, a Ferrari California, Bugatti Veyron, a Porsche Cayenne and an Aston Martin DB11. A testament to the filthy, blood money they'd made from the trafficking. Closer to us, there was a box of tools on a long, well-worn workbench and inside it, I found a crowbar, a range of spanners and screwdrivers, a can of petrol and other items that might be handy in a fight. I saw a vice. Beside it was a toolbox. I saw some aerosol cans of paint and some bottles of antiknock agent. Mechanics used it to sharpen up the fuel efficiency of an engine and as far as automotive chemicals went it was on the more hazardous end of the spectrum. On the skin or in the eyes meant big trouble. I picked up a bottle of it and slipped it inside the barn coat pocket. All good.

"What's that for?" Juliette asked.

"Insurance policy."

She looked around the garage. "Which car do we take?"

"See if any of the cars have keys in the ignition. Vaillancourt probably figured this place is safe. Check the Porsche first. More room for Michelle."

She went off to look at the cars as I made my way over to some tea chests lined up on the back wall. Just interested. I counted three in total. Well-used, battered but strengthened with metal edges, they were neatly lined up and looked out of place. It didn't take three guesses to work out what was inside them, but I left nothing to chance or speculation. I went back to the bench, picked up the crowbar and used it to prise off the first lid. It came away with a soft clunk, half a dozen casing nails protruding dangerously from its outer edge.

Beneath it was a plastic, opaque membrane. I tore it open with the tip of the crowbar and found just what I expected to see. Packed inside a foil-lined chest were some weapons and lots of tidy little bundles of cash. I took one up and thumbed through it. Looked to me like at least ten thousand dollars, crisp and fresh in US fifty-dollar bills, wrapped up together in a nice white currency strap. If all three chests were holding the same illicit cargo, I guessed around fifteen million dollars was waiting for transport. This was the money Duris and Vaillancourt had made trading women like meat to the sickest people in the world.

I heard a car door open and then Juliette walked over

holding some keys. "You got lucky. The Ferrari's keys were inside. Not much room for Michelle."

I looked at her and saw a faint smile of relief. She threw me the keys and looked down at the chest. "What have you found?"

"Looks like some money they're laundering. And also a nice little cache of weapons. Here." I threw her a wad of bills worth ten thousand dollars. "Call it compensation."

She pocketed it without comment. "We need to get going."

"This gets destroyed first."

"How?"

"The only way that always guarantees total destruction. By fire." I handed her the MP5 and told her to put it in the Ferrari. Then I set the Glock down on the workbench and started looking for a way to ignite the cash when I saw a look of horror on Juliette's face.

"Bill," she said, indicating over my shoulder. "Look."

I turned to see Michelle step into the garage. Her face was still and pale with terror. Behind her was a man. As they stepped into the strip-lights, I saw it was Danny Mawson from MI5. "Get behind me, Juliette. Now."

She did that just as Mawson pushed Michelle into the middle of the garage.

"Are you all right, Mimi?" Juliette asked.

Michelle nodded, her face streaked with tears. "I'm sorry,

Bill. He caught me by surprise. Smashed the car window and dragged me out."

"Take it easy," I said.

Mawson laughed. "Take it easy. Yeah, right."

"You're a long way from home, Mawson," I said.

"I'm spending a few days at the British Consulate in Marseille," he said. "And sampling the delights of Provence, as you've seen. And by the way, I cannot believe you snuffed out Duris. Just saw the old man upstairs and gotta say, Blake, that was some sharp shooting. Shame it'll be reported as a heart attack. Now get away from that money. That's coming with me. And step away from the bench. Give that Glock some breathing room."

"All of this for money," I said, stepping back from the Glock. "You disgust me."

"This is not about money," he said, walking over and taking the Glock. "Maybe to the bottom feeders, sure. A few hundred thou here and there, whatever. The people at the top of this operation have all the money they could ever need. For them, this is about power and control. They wind in the political elite like fish, take a nice home video of them being utterly depraved with these women, and then they own them forever. And when I say 'they' I do of course mean 'we'."

"This is an intel operation?" I asked.

He laughed. "Of course it is. Don't be naïve, Blake.

We're talking about wheels within wheels. It's been going on since the dawn of time. This is a big machine, Blake. Bigger than anything you can imagine in your worst nightmares."

"You're lying. I saw you upstairs with them."

"Think of me like a shepherd. I guide these sick old bastards into the pens where they are filmed for posterity and after that, we control everything they do. Their votes, their policies. Two things are going on here, Blake. The trafficking business, that's all theirs. These men buy and sell women around the world and trade them like a commodity. That is their crime. The second thing, the blackmail, that's all ours. The enterprising chaps in the intel community never pass up the opportunity to make hay while the sun shines. Rather than shut this disgusting trade down, we instead choose to exploit it for political gain. Get it now?"

"Then why are you still here?" I asked. "Why come back here and risk taking one of my bullets? Duris and Vaillancourt can't be blackmailed any more."

"Rossi can. He got away."

"But you don't care about that anymore, do you?"

"A pertinent observation."

"Then why come back?"

He shrugged the question away. "Risking my life in the British SIS for the salary I get is not worth all the effort I put in and I consider the pension plan to be a personal insult. Have you any idea how hard it is to watch sums of money like this passing back and forth under your nose all day long and never be able to touch it?"

"My mind does not work like yours, Mawson. So, no."

"Well, it's hard. So, I've decided to check out and take early retirement."

"It is about the money, then."

"Not for the intelligence agencies, but it is for me. Call it a golden handshake."

"I'll call it theft and treachery."

"You say potato..." he laughed. "Anyway, it's neither here nor there what you think, is it now? After you murdered Mulgrave at the country pile, you made yourself an outlaw. A man on the run. Little old me, on the other hand, is another story. My record is unblemished and exemplary. When I deliver your body to the French secret service and they communicate the fact to their colleagues in London, everyone will see the full extent of your treason. Not only a murderer of a British cabinet politician but also a minor player in an international people trafficking ring. I don't imagine The Times will be running an obituary on you, old boy."

I smiled at him. "I'll need a second opinion on that."

Mawson said, "Take as many opinions as you need, but you won't stop me from taking this money and neither will you be closing this operation down. Not ever. What you have uncovered tonight is the proverbial tip of the iceberg.

The rest of the ice is under the water, colder and blacker and deeper than anything you can imagine. You might slow things down for a few days or weeks at best, but then it rises again. The people running this are global players, Blake. They are the real string-pullers, several pay grades above your average world leader or CIA boss. I get away with the cash and vanish forever and sooner or later another trafficking ring starts up. After that, infiltration by intelligence agents is simply a matter of time."

"All just words," I said.

"And what do you care, anyway? They put a kill notice on you." He strolled over to the Cayenne and leaned inside to turn on the ignition. The engine roared to life and started ticking over. "Now, this is how things are going to work out. I've changed my mind about delivering your corpse to the French spooks. Too many questions to answer. Too much bureaucracy. You and these two women will unload the cash from the tea chests and stack it neatly in the back of this Porsche. Then, I will kill all three of you. There will be no evidence of this because after you are dead, I'll drive your bodies over to a meat processing factory that belongs to someone I know. He has a big commercial machine there, an industrial chopper and grinder. All three of you will go into it and never be seen again. Then I'll dump the Porsche, transfer to another vehicle and drive away to someplace nice and warm where I'll never have to wear another pair of socks for the rest of my life."

"And if I don't cooperate?"

He hit a red button on the wall behind him and the shutter doors slowly rolled up, spilling fresh morning light into the garage. "Same thing, but you go into the grinder alive."

I watched his eyes and hands. The eyes were level and calm but the hands were fidgeting.

"What do you say, Blake?"

I said nothing. I wanted the hands to fidget more. I wanted the nerves to show themselves in his eyes. I needed him to panic, to make irrational judgements.

"I asked you a question," he said.

Before I replied, something most extraordinary happened.

FORTY-THREE

Jack Quartermain has a reputation for being fast, silent and bloody. He earned it and he deserves it. The first I knew of his presence in the Vaillancourt villa was when a hand appeared around Mawson's neck. Then there was a wet-crunching noise and I saw the tip of a serrated combat blade protruding from his stomach. Mawson never knew what hit him. Blood ran from his mouth and he stared at me in horror. His mouth worked but no sound came out, then his eyes rolled and he fell off the blade, crashing into the floor with a thud.

Michelle screamed and stepped away, looking down on his dying body with horror and disgust. She tried to move away towards Juliette but the shadow standing behind Mawson grabbed her by the elbow and stopped her. He was a lean, wiry man in black with a navy-blue beanie on his head. He had a scraggly beard and he looked wired.

"All right, Billy," he said.

I moved in front of Juliette. "You took your time, Jack."

Quartermain leaned down and wiped the bloody knife

on Mawson's back. "I don't like to rush a job, me. I don't like nothing to go wrong, neither." He held the blade up and admired the tip. "It's all about the perfect finish."

I stared down at Mawson. He was lying on his stomach on the concrete floor beside a waste bin. His head was turned and he was struggling to breathe. A small pool of black blood was growing around his midriff. I looked at the gaping stab wound in his back and realised Quartermain had twisted the knife. Mawson's shoulders expanded slightly as he took his last breath and then he died. His shoulders contracted as the air seeped from his blood-filled lungs.

I looked into Quartermain's eyes. "Mulgrave is dead, Jack. Operation Taipan died with him. Why not just leave it?"

"Not the way it works, old man."

I tried to think of something to make him see sense, to break his determination to see Taipan through to the end and kill me.

"You can still walk away. You know why I'm here. I'm saving a woman from a people trafficker."

"Stop it. You'll bring a tear to my eye."

"Last chance to let it be, Jack."

He laughed. "You shouldn't have been such a hero, Bill. It was the CCTV cameras at the Gard du Nord that gave you up. We thought maybe you was in America but when the fight broke out on the platform it attracted all sorts of unwanted attention. By the time you turned up to help your damsel in distress here, every lens in the station was on you. Then your ugly mug got flagged by the Interpol system. Next thing you know, I get a day's holiday in Paris, courtesy of the British SIS. All expenses paid. They didn't stretch to five stars though, the bastards. But back to the point. That can happen wherever you are in the world, see. Cameras everywhere. AI algos following you like a bloodhound. There's no stopping a mug like me, boy. I love it, see. I love the chase. I'm a bit partial to spilt blood as well. There's no escape."

"Just because I'm here, with my back against the wall, doesn't mean I'll give up, Jack. You should know that. You've read my file."

"You're against the whole machine, Bill, not just a wall. You won't win. No one wins."

"And what about you? Are you a winner?"

"I'm nothing."

"Just a cog in that machine, eh?"

A bitter laugh. "Maybe, but I've already outlived the great Bill Blake, haven't I?"

"You're counting chickens again, Jack."

"Nah, it's over."

"That remains to be seen."

He took a step closer. "I think not, bud. But for what it's worth, it ain't personal, see. Mawson here was upright filth till I rammed a blade through his middle. I'm not all that happy about his blood being on the soles of my boots, all said and done. They're good boots. Duris, Vaillancourt, Rossi. All vermin. But that's the way of this world of ours. Rossi is someone else's problem. Maybe you done a good job, son. You broke up this disgusting little enterprise and saved some birds from a fate worse than death. Maybe that's a good thing. Maybe not. I dunno. I don't think too hard about stuff like that. It gets in the way of my job."

Without warning, he punched Michelle in the head and knocked her out. It was cold, raw violence and shocking to see. Her young body slumped down as if she was a puppet and someone had cut her strings. In response, Juliette screamed. I ran forward and attacked Quartermain. I'm faster, he's stronger. We play to our advantage. I smacked the blade from his hand and pulled up the same arm, my right hand, into his face, striking his lips and nose with the back of my hand. Maybe I broke the nose. Hard to say. He grunted in pain and pushed me away and reached out and grabbed my hand.

He rotated around in a corkscrew motion and pulled my arm around his body so it was gripped in his hands in front of him but I was behind him. I felt him forcing my hand inside something cold and metallic and worked out fast it was the bench vice I'd seen next to the toolbox. He began winding the handle to trap my hand between the static and sliding jaws. I guessed the plan was either to crush it to mush or trap me in there to give him enough time to inflict some other damage on me. I considered the antiknock agent in my pocket but couldn't reach it. I had a second to act and only one move to make. Moving around to the side as far as I could go, I headbutted him in the side of his head, aiming for the pterion, the weakest bone in the skull.

It worked, but hurt me too, almost knocking me out. Dizzy and shocked, I was only dimly aware of Quartermain falling away to the floor. This gave me enough time to unwind the handle and free my hand from the vice. But my opponent wasn't down for long. He sprang up like a devil and charged at me with a wild look in his eyes.

FORTY-FOUR

I had only one play. And that was to dip down and run into him, using his centre of mass against him and executing a perfect dump tackle, smacking him down on his backside. He reached out to grab me as I clambered off him, so I grabbed his wrist and rotated it around, snapping the bones. He cried out as I scrambled for the blade but he was already on his feet and kicked it away under the Aston, unflinching, even with his wounds. I needed another weapon but the MP5 was on the other side of the garage in the Ferrari and the Glock was squashed under Mawson's dead body, also too far away. One option came to mind; the tea chest lid. It was near to hand and dangerous. I picked it up and weighed it. Not enough to do any real damage, but that depended on how inventive I was. I pulled it back and slashed it through the air sideways for maximum speed, then brought the side with the casing nails down hard in his face. I felt one of the nails bury itself in his cheek, and then pulled the lid down hard, ripping open a deep, long gouge in his face.

He screamed in pain, almost unable to believe what had

just happened. His confusion gave me another second to think. I used the time to rotate the plywood lid until it was metal edge-on and piled it forward into his throat, crushing his windpipe and sending him to his knees, gasping mouth and bulging eyes. Last act, I brought my boot up and kicked him in the chin, aiming for the other side of Marseille. His head cracked back against his spine and he tumbled over onto his side, slipping on Mawson's blood, knocked out as cold as ice in a pile of junk in the corner.

I threw the lid down on him and pulled the Glock out from under Mawson. After cleaning it up, I checked it was still in working order. I also executed a rapid combat reload of the mag in case the drop had caused any problems I didn't want to deal with in a fire fight. Then I walked over to Michelle. A visibly shocked Juliette also ran over to her.

"She's okay, I think," I said. "It was a hard blow but she's still breathing. Watch her while I finish up."

I gave Juliette the Glock and told her to keep it trained on Quartermain while I walked over to the shelves at the back of the garage and found the petrol can I'd seen on my way in. I took hold of it and walked over to the chests.

"Bill, it's Mimi," Juliette called over. "She's coming around. She's all right."

"Good."

Back over at the tea chests, I prised off the other two lids, tipped a good few glugs of petrol over the cash and tossed the can. It was then I saw movement in my peripheral vision.

I turned to see Quartermain, his face all smashed in, climbing out from the junk pile and lunging towards me. I'd put the gun away to go through the chests and as I fumbled for it, he leapt at me and grabbed me by the throat.

"I'll kill you now, you bastard," he screamed, eyes bulging and blood running from the wound on his cheek.

I brought my hands up and tried to force him off me, but Quartermain is a very strong man, almost freakishly so. Lean, wiry, and pure road-tested muscle. As he choked me, I began to cough and splutter and feel the blood rushing to my head. Things began to fade out.

Until the gunshot.

A loud, almost deafening blast from a nine-mil being fired somewhere to my right. My ear was ringing due to the proximity of the explosion. I smelt the smoke at the same time Quartermain rolled off me, grunting in pain. I staggered up to my feet and saw a dazed and weary Michelle, sitting up on the floor in front of the doorway, holding a shaking Glock in her two hands, arms outstretched, and her face frozen in a rictus of fear and disgust. She must have taken the gun from her sister when she saw Quartermain choking me. Juliette was standing beside her, hands clamped over her ears and tears streaming down her cheeks.

I glanced at Quartermain. He was still. I moved over to her and took the gun. "Are you okay?"

She shook her head. "No."

I saw she was all right, physically if not mentally. As Juliette slowly nursed her back to reality, I noticed movement in the chrome hubcaps of the Porsche Cayenne and spun around to see Quartermain had staggered to his feet once again. It looked like Michelle had shot him through the upper leg and he was cradling his broken wrist like it was a dying bird. As he sidled over to the Bugatti, he looked me in the eye and smiled.

"Not half bad, Colonel. I'll give you that."

I raised the gun I had taken from Michelle and aimed to kill him, but he was gone, inside the Veyron and out of the garage. I fired on the speeding car, striking the front wing twice and the windscreen three times as he reversed the vehicle at speed. Then he spun the wheel, turning the car in a tight arc, changed into first gear and disappeared down the winding drive. He was gone.

"Do we go after him?" Michelle asked.

"No, absolutely not," I said. "We let him go."

"But he'll come back to kill you!"

"That is my problem, not yours. Besides, I have a plan to handle him."

Then I took four bundles of cash from the nearest tea chest, pocketing one and igniting the other three with my lighter and tossed one into each of the chests.

They went up with a deep whoofing noise and in seconds

the garage was filling up with noxious black smoke. Once things got really out of control down here, the petrol tanks in the other cars would also go up. That would rock the place, but how the partygoers got out was their problem.
"Get in the Cayenne," I said to them both. "We're out of here."

FORTY-FIVE

The autoroute stretched away to the northern horizon and the Cayenne cruised along nicely under a warm French sun. An Eighties hit was playing on the radio and Michelle and Juliette spoke quietly in the back seat. I could see Juliette had been through a lot. Someone had given her a black eye and she had other marks and bruises, but she looked fundamentally unhurt. Michelle had a concussion from the blow to her head, but most of her wounds were inside her mind. Time would heal both women.

Up ahead, the southern banlieues of Paris began to make themselves known in the distance. Except for a stop in a small town north of Lyon to visit a bank, we'd been driving non-stop for hours and left Provence long behind us. The midday news had reported the untimely and tragic death of Nicolas Duris in a housefire at Max Vaillancourt's villa. There was no mention of a party or any other guests. It was like none of them had ever existed.

I navigated through the southern suburbs of Paris with one eye on the dashboard clock. My appointment with Louis

Virkler was rapidly approaching. I knew if I was late one more time he'd ghost me in the most total of fashions. Good old Louis. I drove past Sénart Forest and into the city at Crigny. We drove through Massy and Montrouge and cruised along the east bank of the Seine until we reached Juliette's apartment in Grenelle. It was on the top floor of a building on the Rue Desaix. Tall sash windows and an ornamental balcony. Just the sort of place an intelligent, successful investigative journalist like Juliette Dupont would choose to live. Nice.

She thanked me and walked inside, telling her sister she would see her in a moment. Michelle was outside the car now and walked around and leaned into the driver's window.

"You're not coming inside for coffee, are you?"

I smiled. "Sorry, but..."

"You have somewhere to be, I know, I know. You never did tell me what that was all about."

"I just need to see a man about a dog."

She looked confused. "What?"

"An old English saying. It means I'm not going to tell you where I'm going or what I'm doing. It's not personal. You don't need to know and it would only put you in danger."

"You lead one hell of a life, Bill."

"So they say, and yet all I want to do is settle down."

"You can come and work on our vineyard if you like. I

talked Juliette into it on the drive up here. You seem to be the sort of man who can get things done."

"Thanks, but no thanks. I might visit you there one day."

"That would be good. To meet up again in better circumstances." She paused for a long time, looking up at the apartment and then back down to me. "Are we going to be safe now?"

I nodded. "They're all gone now, Michelle. Manu, Rüdiger, Gobet, Diouf, Vaillancourt. Even Duris. All of them. They're dead and their entire trafficking circle is smashed. They can't come back from the grave."

She nodded but said nothing, her smile fading. "Goodbye, then."

"Au revoir, Michelle."

She stepped back from the car and I pulled away. By the time I was at the end of the street, I'd hit the speed dial and was calling an old friend. Seconds later, a cool, calm voice picked up the call.

"Good evening, Colonel Blake."

"Richard. Hi."

"So, it's first names now, is it?"

"Sparrowhawk was always too cool for a desk jockey like you."

He laughed, but it faded fast. "Did you get him? I heard about the fire."

He wanted me to tell him that Quartermain was dead,

that his brother's brutal murder had been avenged and it was all over. I wanted to be able to say that, too, but I couldn't. "He got away, Richard. He got out of the villa before the place went up."

A long pause. "Damn it."

"I wounded him pretty badly, so he'll have to get patched up somewhere."

"He'll come back to England. D19 is being pulled back together. He knows people on the inside. I'll tell you now, the new management is restructuring things not necessarily to your advantage. And as far as Quartermain is concerned, Taipan will remain an active order until you're terminated."

I was driving the car along the Rue de Belgrade, and now crossing the Avenue de la Bourdonnais and steering into the back streets of Gros-Caillou. "That was my impression after the short chat I had with him back in Marseille. I presume there's a D Notice on all reporting about the people trafficking ring."

"You presume correctly. Senior politicians from all over Europe are involved, including the UK. None of it will ever see the light of day. But then, you knew that before you decided to help the Dupont woman."

"I did," I said, pulling up into a narrow cobblestone backroad and rolling to a gentle stop outside a terraced house with filthy white shutters over the windows. Metal poles had been erected down one side of the street to stop parking, but this side was residents' parking only. Virkler had already told me to use his space. I would have done it anyway. I switched the engine off and unbuckled my belt, letting it quietly roll back through the pillar loop.

After a long pause, he said, "You learn anything over the last twenty-four hours, Blake?"

"That igniting fifteen million dollars isn't as much fun as you might think."

He was silent for a few seconds. "You did what?"

"Perhaps another time. Right now, I have some business to attend to."

"Don't tell me, it's confidential."

"You read my mind."

"I think I'm starting to get to know you, Bill."

"Nobody knows me, Richard. Goodbye."

I cut the call and climbed out of the Porsche.

FORTY-SIX

I buzzed the door and the reply was instant. "Colonel, how nice of you to call. You have less than twenty minutes to spare. You like to cut things fine."

"Open the door, Louis."

"Up the steps on the right."

I heard a clunk and it popped open. I stepped inside. A small interior courtyard presented itself to me, with some dead plants in pots sitting on the same cobblestones that made the street outside. The stairs were beside a birdcage lift, which I decided to give a miss. Instead, I climbed the steps on the right. I had the Glock in the barn coat's pocket. I was kind of getting used to it being there if I'm honest. I didn't think I'd end up using it, but when it came to men like Virkler, you always play things nice and cool. At the top of the steps was another door, ajar. I tapped on it and it opened right up. Already open.

"Welcome to my home, Colonel."

I stepped in and closed the door with a quiet, weak click. Louis Virkler was standing on the other side of the room behind a desk stacked high with clutter. A hole-punch, staplegun, a pot of pens, broken pencils, passport printing plates, visa stamps, specialist inks and topping it all off, a Selmer Paris clarinet and finally an old Anglepoise lamp balanced on top of a pile of newspapers.

"Bonjour, Louis," I said. "Comment ça va?"

"Your French isn't bad. It isn't good, but isn't bad."

"Thanks. Have you got the package?"

"Of course."

Virkler leant forwards and opened a drawer. I refrained from reaching for the Glock, but I was thinking about it. As it turned out, there was no need. He straightened himself back up and walked around the desk with a thick Jiffy envelope in his hands. He handed it to me.

"Here."

"Thanks."

"Anything for an old friend and a good customer. You owe me two thousand American dollars."

I reached into my jacket. Not for the gun, but for money I'd taken from the chest back in Marseille. "That's some inflation, Louis. Your prices are going up faster than Max Vaillancourt's villa."

He eyed me. "You did that?"

"I have no idea what you're talking about."

I handed him the cash and checked out his work while he counted the money. It was very fine work, as usual. I looked at Virkler. He was a snake among men. You never told him more than you had to. "Thanks for the work you did on the passport. It's second to none."

He shrugged, his face becoming affable and innocent like a lost child. Then, he offered me a deep, Gallic shrug. "Why do you think people put up with my attitude?"

"Nonetheless, your work is as excellent as ever. Good name, too. William Bonham."

He held up one of the dollar bills to the window. "These are good, too. It's a pleasure doing business with you." He looked at the passport. "Where are you flying away to, Mr Bonham?"

I was glad Virkler had asked. If he hadn't asked, I would have had to find a way to drop my next sentence into the conversation and that might have looked like I was planting a seed. This way was much better. This was a much more organic way for Quartermain to find out where I was when he beat the information out of Virkler. You see, everyone in my line of work knows Louis Virkler. Everyone includes Jack Quartermain. The first thing a man like Quartermain does when he finds out I've fled Europe is to visit Louis Virkler and ask some questions. He might ask them nicely, he might ask them rudely. He might get very violent. That was all Virkler's problem – an everyday hazard in his line of work.

I set down the first breadcrumb as carefully and as

casually as I could.

"I'm flying away to the United States of America, Louis. I need to settle an old account in Arizona."

He weighed that up. "And what's in Arizona?"

I stuffed the new passport in the barn coat. "Three pounds of hate and an ounce of revenge."

"That sounds like trouble to me. Who's the lucky person?"

"Let's just say that someone who hurt me very much is about to learn the true meaning of the word payback."

I said nothing more. I turned and walked away, closing the door behind me and making my way down the smoked wood stairs that snaked around the birdcage lift outside the apartment. I moved quickly across the small courtyard and out into the street where I climbed into the Porsche. It was a long drive across the city to Charles de Gaulle Airport and I had a flight to catch.

AUTHOR'S NOTE

The quotation at the start of this book was written in 1942 by Albert Camus, who was killed twenty-one years later in a car crash when he was forty-six. His original French is '*Ce qui m'intéresse en ce moment, c'est d'échapper à la mécanique*' meaning to escape from the 'mechanic' or mechanics, a reference to the machinery of justice, ultimately the guillotine. If you enjoyed this novel, please consider leaving a rating or a short Amazon review at the following link. Thank you.

Website: www.robjonesnovels.com

Facebook: www.facebook.com/RobJonesNovels/

Email: robjonesnovels@gmail.com

Twitter: @AuthorRobJones

Printed in Great Britain
by Amazon

27148175R00158